FIRST SURRENDER

THE SERAFINA: SIN CITY SERIES

Katie Reus

Cover art: Jaycee of Sweet 'N Spicy Designs
Author website: http://www.katiereus.com

First Surrender/Katie Reus. -- 1st ed.

ISBN-10: 1942447442
ISBN-13: 9781942447443

eISBN: 9780989776608

For my readers.

Praise for the novels of Katie Reus

"...an engrossing page-turner that I enjoyed in one sitting. Reus offers all the ingredients I love in a paranormal romance."
—Book Lovers, Inc.

"Has all the right ingredients: a hot couple, evil villains, and a killer action-filled plot. . . . [The] Moon Shifter series is what I call Grade-A entertainment!"
—Joyfully Reviewed

"I could not put this book down. . . . Let me be clear that I am not saying that this was a good book *for* a paranormal genre; it was an excellent romance read, *period.*" —All About Romance

"Reus strikes just the right balance of steamy sexual tension and nail-biting action....This romantic thriller reliably hits every note that fans of the genre will expect." —*Publishers Weekly*

"Prepare yourself for the start of a great new series! . . . I'm excited about reading more about this great group of characters."
—Fresh Fiction

"Nonstop action, a solid plot, good pacing and riveting suspense..."
—RT Book Reviews (4.5 Stars)

"Wow! This powerful, passionate hero sizzles with sheer deliciousness. I loved every sexy twist of this fun & exhilarating tale. Katie Reus delivers!" —Carolyn Crane, RITA award winning author

Continued...

"You'll fall in love with Katie's heroes."
—*New York Times* bestselling author, Kaylea Cross

"A sexy, well-crafted paranormal romance that succeeds with smart characters and creative world building." —Kirkus Reviews

"*Mating Instinct*'s romance is taut and passionate . . . Katie Reus's newest installment in her Moon Shifter series will leave readers breathless!"
—Stephanie Tyler, *New York Times* bestselling author

"Reus has definitely hit a home run with this series. . . . This book has mystery, suspense, and a heart-pounding romance that will leave you wanting more."
—Nocturne Romance Reads

"Katie Reus pulls the reader into a story line of second chances, betrayal, and the truth about forgotten lives and hidden pasts."
—The Reading Café

"If you are looking for a really good, new military romance series, pick up *Targeted*! The new Deadly Ops series stands to be a passionate and action-riddled read."
—That's What I'm Talking About

"Sexy suspense at its finest."
—Laura Wright, *New York Times* bestselling author of *Branded*

CHAPTER ONE

Sierra took a subtle sniff of her upper arm as she rode the elevator up to the fiftieth floor of the new Serafina hotel and casino—owned by billionaire Wyatt Christiansen. As head chef at Cloud 9, one of the restaurants at the Serafina, she sometimes smelled like food at the end of a long shift even though she'd changed clothes. Okay, she always smelled like food. Which wasn't necessarily a bad thing, but she'd cooked a lot of seafood today. She didn't scent anything too strong but was sure her friend Hayden would tell her when she saw him. At least she'd changed out of her work clothes and chef's coat so she was comfortable in jeans and a fitted T-shirt.

He'd started work at the Serafina the same time she had. It had officially opened a year ago. She'd been brought over from one of Christiansen's other hotels to work here and Hayden had been hired after retiring from the Navy. Christiansen's wife Iris ran all the security at the hotel, but Hayden was directly under her as her second-in-command. Sierra didn't know how they handled the stress of security at such a mammoth hotel. She'd go cross-eyed trying to watch all those cameras at once. But, they had a good team with minimum problems.

As the elevator dinged, announcing her arrival to the security floor, damn butterflies took flight in her stomach. It always happened when she was about to see Hayden and she hated it. When she'd first met him, she thought he was a big jerk. A big, scary jerk. Okay, a sexy-as-hell jerk with tattooed sleeves covering both his arms. His tats added to that whole tall, dark and intimidating thing he had going on. As a former SEAL, Hayden certainly had the training for his current profession. But she'd come to learn that he was one of the sweetest men she'd ever known. For the last year they'd hung out constantly as friends and Thursday nights they had a standing ritual of dinner, drinks and sometimes she coerced him into going dancing with her and her friends. Usually he just stood guard by one of their tables and growled at any males who got too close. Which made her adore him even more.

God, she really was a masochist. Hayden was never going to be interested in her romantically but that didn't stop her from wanting him more and more every day. Hayden could have any woman he wanted and she knew she didn't fit the mold of his type. It was her freaking curse in life. Growing up and in college she had a lot of male friends because of her 'friendly' personality but she never dated any of them. One of her college friends had told her that she was way too 'the girl next door type', the type of girl you brought home to your mother—which was freaking annoying. She wanted to be the type of girl who got a man's pulse pounding out of control. The kind who got him so hot and bothered that he couldn't think straight. But not just any man. Only Hayden.

Her flat sandals snapped softly against the marble as she entered the security floor. A giant glass wall greeted her. Behind it she could see desks, and too many television screens to count. Some huge, some small, focused on dealers' hands, patrons, the various bars and pretty much anywhere legal a camera could go. The array of them still astounded her. Stopping at one of the glass doors, she placed her hand on the biometric scanner. Once it scanned her palm, the door immediately opened with a whoosh. She had no business up here but about eight months ago Hayden had programmed her into the system so she wouldn't have to bug him every Thursday. Sometimes she got off earlier than him and preferred to wait in the security room as opposed to the bar in her restaurant. She was there enough during the week; she didn't want to hang out in her off time too.

Stepping inside she was inundated with noise and frantic chatter. Men and women were talking into their headsets, some clearly worried. There was normally a fast pace up here but today it seemed different.

Glancing around, Sierra didn't see Hayden anywhere but assumed he was in his office. Before she'd taken two steps in that direction, Marty, one of the tech guys, jumped up from his desk when he saw her. "Hey, honey. What are you doing up here?"

She normally didn't like nicknames but Marty called every female honey. She smiled. "Just stopping by to see if Hayden could sneak away early."

Marty's eyes widened slightly. "Oh...he's not here. He said something about a date."

A date? The word was like a punch to her gut. For a moment she was totally stunned, but she wasn't going to show it in front of anyone, especially not a coworker. This place was worse than a middle school when it came to gossip. So she pasted on a smile. "Oh, right. He mentioned that, I totally forgot."

Marty started to respond but Iris Christiansen strode through the glass doorway looking fierce in black pants, a crisp white button down shirt and a sleek, clearly custom-made black jacket. Everything about the other woman was, well, fierce. She was gorgeous but also a little scary, especially since Sierra knew the former Marine was always well-armed. The tall woman gave Marty one look and he scampered away.

Luckily she gave Sierra a bright smile. "What's up, Sierra? You got a problem at the restaurant?"

Still struggling to find her voice, she shook her head. "No problem, just leaving. See you tomorrow." Sierra tried to hurry away, but Iris followed her to the elevators.

"What's going on? You don't look okay."

Sierra swallowed hard. Lord, was she that transparent? "Just had a long day. Busy, you know?" *Gah, why wouldn't the elevator hurry up?*

Iris raised a dark eyebrow. "Do I need to kick his ass?"

Staring at her, Sierra frowned. "What? Who?"

"Hayden. What's he done now?"

The mention of his name made Sierra's stomach flip-flop. It also pissed her off. If he'd had a date he could have had the decency to tell her. Shrugging jerkily, she breathed out a sigh of relief when the elevator stopped and dinged. "Hayden hasn't done anything." And she wondered why Iris would assume this had anything to do with the man. It wasn't like they were dating.

Iris didn't respond, but her lips pulled into a thin line as the doors shut behind Sierra. Once she was alone, Sierra didn't bother to keep up a happy face. Hayden hadn't mentioned dating anyone in the past year, though she knew the man had to be dating. He was walking, talking sex appeal. Absently she rubbed the center of her chest. So, he was dating. No big deal. Right? Ugh, yeah right. Swallowing back the traitorous tears threatening to overwhelm her, she hurried into the below ground parking garage. Normally Hayden or someone else walked her to her vehicle but she didn't want to bother asking anyone else. Not when she felt like crying. No way was she embarrassing herself and becoming a source of casino gossip.

Picking up her pace, her sandals slapped quickly across the concrete. As she reached the second row of cars, a tiny scream escaped her lips as a man wearing a mask jumped out from behind her Jeep. The guy was huge, maybe six feet tall, and when she saw the flash of metal—a knife!—in his hands, her chest constricted as a hundred horrible scenarios raced through her mind. Knowing she'd only get one chance she let out a blood-curdling scream at the top of her lungs as she backtracked and started running in the other direction.

Blood rushed in her ears as she continued screaming and digging in her purse for her pepper spray. She knew she wouldn't be a physical match against anyone and—pain exploded in her scalp as he grabbed her by the hair and jerked back.

Instinctively she reached back to try to stop him and quickly realized her mistake. Using a lot of force, he slammed her forehead against a nearby car. Another burst of pain launched inside her skull as she tried to shove away from the vehicle. He pulled her head back again and she struggled to find breath—suddenly she was falling.

"Hey! Stop!" An angry male voice ricocheted off the walls of the parking garage and she heard multiple sets of footsteps pounding against the pavement as her palms hit the ground.

Rolling over, she raised her hands instinctively to fight off another blow but found Jay, Hayden's brother, racing toward her. It was hard to see because of the tears blurring her vision but he was hard to miss.

She struggled to stand but stopped and just sagged against the vehicle, thankful someone had been there to scare off her attacker. The side of her head ached but she didn't even care. Closing her eyes, she let her head fall back against the vehicle and didn't bother to fight the tears that poured out. When she thought about what could have happened...a sob wracked her body as she wrapped her arms around herself.

CHAPTER TWO

"Come *on,*" Hayden muttered to his computer screen as it powered down. He wanted to get the fuck out of here and meet up with Sierra. Glancing at his cell, he frowned when he saw the time and started to text her. Normally he didn't bother her during working hours because she was just as busy as him and could barely look at her phone, but she should be off by now. As he started punching in letters, the glass door to his office opened.

Iris, his direct boss, stepped in looking pissed. At him. His eyebrows raised. He'd seen Iris angry at a lot of people, namely jackasses who'd tried to rob the place, but her ire had never been aimed at him. Before he could ask what was going on, she turned and snapped the shades down on the window to his office. It overlooked part of the security area, giving everyone open access to him and vice versa.

After giving them privacy, she dropped into one of the chairs in front of his desk. "What's going on with Sierra?"

That stopped him cold. Had something happened? Ice chilled his veins. "What do you mean?"

Iris's dark eyes narrowed accusingly. "I just saw her leaving and she looked upset. She tried to cover it, but she wears her emotions right out in the open. I swear if you hurt that girl—"

Hayden held up his hands. "What the hell, Iris? I'd *never* hurt Sierra." He'd rather cut off his own arm than cause her pain.

Iris immediately relaxed. "Okay, I figured you didn't do anything but had to be sure. We can't afford to lose her—I'd kill you for that alone. That woman can freaking cook."

Hayden rolled his eyes. Iris ate at Sierra's restaurant at least once a day, and he didn't know where the slim woman put it all. That wasn't what he cared about though. "So wait, Sierra was *here* and left?" They had a standing 'date' every Thursday night. It was his favorite night of the week even if it wasn't a real date. He wished it was though. The kind where she ended up back at his place, naked and underneath him as he pumped into her for hours. He needed to get over his bullshit and just make a move. It was hard though, because if he read her wrong and she rejected him—that thought pierced him in a way he couldn't even think about.

Iris nodded, her expression curious as she watched him.

Ignoring her for the moment, he picked up his phone and started to call Sierra when it rang. It was his brother. He picked up on the first ring. "Hey."

"I'm in parking garage B, section 210. Get your ass down here. Sierra's been hurt," Jay said hurriedly.

The words were like a punch to his system. Hayden jumped up and motioned for Iris to follow. Time seemed to slow down and everything around him sharpened into focus as they hurried toward the elevators. "How bad? What happened?" The thought of anything happening to Sierra...fuck, he couldn't even go there. Before he heard all the facts he needed to keep a level head.

"Someone attacked her, slammed her head against a car. She's got some bruising and she's upset but otherwise physically unharmed. The fucker got away because I had to check on her first. By the time I went after him there was no trace of him. The paramedics and police are on their way but I've got someone...hold on..." In the background he could hear Jay murmuring something then he was back on the line. "Listen, if you see Iris—"

"She's with me," he said as they stepped into the elevator. "We'll be there in less than a minute."

"Good."

As they disconnected, Hayden shoved his phone in his pants pocket. He quickly relayed what his brother had told him as the elevator started moving. He slid his master key into the panel so they would go directly to the parking garage. The ride was fast but it seemed like the longest minute of his entire life. As a former SEAL, he'd been on a shit-load of brutal missions in war-torn countries, been stuck behind enemy lines with no backup for days, but nothing compared to the fear pumping through his veins now. Not only was Sierra the sweetest, most sensual woman he knew, she fucking owned him. Even if she didn't know it yet.

"Your brother said she's unhurt," Iris murmured, her voice unusually soft.

Hayden couldn't even respond. His vocal cords refused to work. After what felt like an eternity, the door finally opened and he raced out. Half a dozen men in security uniforms were standing guard, giving Sierra and Jay a ten foot radius. Hayden was sure his brother or someone had already started the hunt for whoever had tried to hurt her. Normally he'd take over the situation, but all he cared about was making sure Sierra was safe. He would deal with hunting down and destroying whoever had attacked her later.

CHAPTER THREE

Sierra's eyes widened when she saw Hayden barreling down on her and Jay. Her head throbbed, but Jay had gotten an ice pack for her which helped. Now they were waiting on the police so she could fill out a report. She'd have to make an official one at the casino too, but none of that concerned her now.

The craziest sense of relief pumped through her now that Hayden was here. She was still hurt that he'd apparently been going on some date, but she was grateful for his presence. At six feet five he was a freaking giant compared to her. Something she teased him about occasionally. Normally he wore a suit and tie to work but at the moment he just had on dark slacks and a buttoned up white shirt. His sleeves were rolled up, showing off his tattooed, incredibly muscular arms. Everything about him was big, intimidating and sexy.

Ignoring his brother, Hayden didn't stop until he was right in front of her, completely crowding her personal space. Even though she was standing, he had to bend down because of her shorter height. He cupped the left side of her head, gently rubbing his thumb over her cheek as he turned her head to look at the damage on the right side. She was too stunned by his touch to even think about protesting. Words caught in her throat as he lifted the ice pack away and made a low, menacing sound in his throat.

After a moment he turned her back so that she had to look directly at him. There were so many emotions in his gaze and he was still rubbing her cheek in a soft, sensual way that made all her pain fade. He'd never touched her like this before. Sure, they'd hugged and he occasionally slung an arm around her shoulders in a friendly way but this felt different somehow. Either that or she'd hit her head harder than she thought. It was probably the head thing.

"How're you feeling, baby?" he rasped out.

She blinked in shock. *Baby?* Her mouth partially opened as he leaned closer. For a moment she thought he was going to kiss her, but then she realized he was looking at her eyes. Of course he was. She felt like an idiot for thinking otherwise. He was trying to check if she had a concussion.

"Are you nauseated?" he asked quietly.

The concern she saw in his face was almost enough to make her burst into tears. She was trying to keep it together but with him there it was damn hard. "No."

"Did you lose consciousness?"

Jay had already asked her these questions but she just shook her head. "No."

"Are you feeling dizzy or tired? Do you hear a ringing in your ears?"

"No to all of the above."

"What about a headache?"

"Of course I have a headache. Someone slammed my head against a car." She tried to keep her words light, but her voice cracked on the last word.

Hayden swore softly before gathering her against his chest. He wrapped his huge arms around her and even though she knew it was a mistake, she slid her arms around him and laid the uninjured side of her head against his chest. That masculine, raw scent that drove her crazy twined around her, soothing her as much as his hold did. Right now she needed his strength and wasn't afraid to admit it.

"What do you know so far?" Hayden asked Jay.

"Someone wearing a black mask attacked her. She screamed, tried to run, and he caught up with her. Slammed her against that car," he said as he pointed to it. "It was just by chance I was down here too. I scared him off. I wanted to go after him but I couldn't leave her alone."

"I'm going to fucking kill him." There was such rage in Hayden's voice that Sierra stepped back. He was always in such tight control of his emotions, even when dealing with would-be thieves and criminals at the casino. Nothing ever ruffled him so to hear his voice practically shaking was a shock.

He wouldn't fully let her go though, sliding his hands lower and keeping them firmly on her hips. "Hayden, no, the police are on their way. They'll handle this. But I don't understand how anyone got in here. Unless..." Oh God, why hadn't she thought of that? It had to be an employee. "Someone from the casino did this?" An uncontrollable shudder snaked through her.

"Not necessarily," Iris said as she strode up. Sierra had seen her arrive with Hayden but the head of hotel security had been talking on her phone in hurried, but hushed tones. "I just got off the phone with one of the tech guys. Turns out there was a glitch in the system. Two of the doors down here were unlocked because of it and...the video feed was off too."

Sierra's blood chilled at the words. Next to her, Hayden stiffened, so she knew she wasn't crazy. The locks in the garage were electric so she could see a mistake happening if there was a computer error, but for the video feed to malfunction too... "The video just in this garage or everywhere?"

Iris cleared her throat. "Just this section of the garage."

Which meant this had been somewhat planned. Maybe she hadn't been the specific target, but the security at the Serafina was vigilant about having eyes everywhere, especially when it concerned the safety of their employees. It was one of the reasons Sierra loved working at the casino.

"I don't believe in coincidences," Hayden said.

Iris and Jay murmured an agreement as Sierra tried to wrap her mind around what had happened. It still seemed too surreal and she was just so damn grateful to be relatively unharmed. Things could have been a hell of a lot worse. Over the last month Sierra had fired multiple employees. Some for stealing, others for using drugs on the premises. It wasn't completely out of the realm of possibilities that someone had targeted her because of that. While she wanted to believe the best of people, she'd seen people do stupid stuff when they were desperate or felt wronged.

"I'm having a full systems check and analysis run on our security right now to figure out why we had a glitch with the locks. And you better believe I'll find out what happened to that feed. This kind of thing won't happen again," Iris said.

"I want all the names of the people Sierra fired since the opening of the Serafina. We'll focus on them first, and if we can't narrow it down we might expand our suspect pool." There was no denying the underlying rage in Hayden's voice. If anything, he seemed even angrier than a few moments before.

The sound of sirens getting near made Sierra wince, but she kept her focus on Hayden. "What about the police?"

"Tell them everything you know. They'll investigate but so will we. That fucker better hope the cops get to him first." He didn't look away from her as he spoke, a silent promise in his eyes that slightly terrified her.

Not because she was afraid of him. Sierra had always known Hayden was a badass. His military record was enough to prove that, but right now she felt like she was seeing him for the first time. Or at least the true warrior lurking beneath the surface. Before she could respond, Jay cut in.

"Shut it, Hayden. Don't let the cops hear you saying that shit," his brother muttered at the sound of screeching tires and slamming doors. Sierra looked toward the end of the row of nearest line of cars.

There were three marked and two unmarked police cars. A man she recognized as a detective from another problem they'd had at the casino strode toward them wearing a stony expression. Sierra wanted to bury her face against Hayden's chest and block everything out, but knew it was impossible. So she stepped back, ready to get the questioning and paperwork over with, but Hayden snagged an arm around her waist and pulled her close. His fingers dug into her hips, urging her to stay near.

Okay, then. She wasn't inclined to fight him, but she was surprised by his actions. Usually he was careful about not touching her too much. She sighed and sidled up next to him. The man was a complete rock, all hardness and muscles and raw strength. She could really feel it now too. Once all this insanity was ironed out she'd be going home alone so she wanted to take advantage of the support he was offering now.

*****

"You finally going to make your move?" Jay asked quietly as he and Hayden stood near a concrete pillar out of the way of the police and the paramedics who were talking to Sierra.

Hayden crossed his arms over his chest, hating the helpless sensation he experienced as he watched Sierra shaking her head at something one of the paramedics said. Her arms were wrapped tightly around her middle and her shoulders were hunched, making her look even more fragile than normal. Her long midnight black hair was pulled up into a ponytail and after a long day of work she didn't have much makeup left. Even pale, tired and practically shaking, she was the sexiest woman he'd ever known. It wasn't just her looks—though there was no arguing she was beautiful, even if she didn't seem to realize it—she had the biggest heart of anyone he'd ever met.

When he'd started work at the Serafina, he'd had a chip on his shoulder the size of Texas. He'd been surly, not liking the direction his life had taken him. His brother Jay had left the Navy because a team of his men had died. Then Jay had gotten a job working directly for Wyatt Christiansen.

Hayden had left the Navy because he'd had to. And he'd been fucking pissed about it, even after he'd gotten such a prime position. He hadn't been grateful to find such a well-paying job close to his only family. No, he'd focused on the negative. Until he'd met Sierra. She'd told him to stop acting like a dick about something he'd said or done, and he hadn't been able to tell her to fuck off. He was a Southern boy through and through and never would have said that to a woman anyway, but Sierra had made him feel like shit. And he'd deserved it.

Everything had changed from that first meeting with her. It had been subtle at first, but now he was so damn grateful to be able to do another job he enjoyed. Working in the same vicinity of the woman he...damn, he couldn't even admit the words to himself. Rubbing the middle of this chest, Hayden realized Jay was staring at him.

"What?" he snapped.

"I asked you a question. You gonna make a move on her or what? There's a pool going on how long it's going to take you and if you wait another week, I'll win."

"Man, fuck you," he muttered, not missing the good-natured smile Jay gave him.

Hayden wasn't sure if his brother was joking about the pool or not, but there was one thing he knew for sure. He wasn't waiting any longer. After what had just happened to Sierra, he was letting her know how he felt.

"I'm not coming in tomorrow and neither is she. Probably not the day after either," Hayden said quietly, making sure no one overheard them. He knew it would take some convincing, but there was no way he was letting Sierra go home alone tonight. And forget about coming in to work tomorrow.

"You taking her back to your place?"

"Yeah...if she'll go."

"She will." There was a certainty in his brother's voice that Hayden didn't feel. "I know you want to be hands on with this, but Iris and the rest of the team have this covered. They'll find out what the hell is going on. In the meantime, Sierra doesn't need to be here. If this was a targeted attack on her..." Jay trailed off, not bothering to fill in what Hayden already knew.

Keeping her far away from the Serafina and under his roof was the smartest thing they could do for her.

When the detective and paramedics let Sierra go, he watched as she scanned the garage. She stopped when she saw him, relief lighting up her pale face. His body tensed with all her focus on him. "We'll leave her car here, but keep it under surveillance. I've got my phone. Call me for anything."

Jay grunted, likely because he or Iris had already planned to do just that. Hayden hurried toward Sierra, his shoes silent against the concrete. She still had her arms wrapped around her middle when she stopped in front of him.

"They're not making me go down to the station," she said, even though Hayden already knew they wouldn't. Normally it was protocol but Iris had called in a favor for Sierra. Something he greatly appreciated. "And I'm not going to the hospital. They can't do anything for me." The way she said it sounded as if she expected him to argue.

Hayden nodded because he understood. It was unlikely she had anything more than a mild concussion—and he didn't think she even had that. The bruising and swelling would heal on their own. "I don't blame you. Do you have everything you need to leave?"

Frowning, she nodded and patted her purse. "Uh, yeah."

"Good, you're coming home with me. We can stop by your place and grab a bag of clothes, but I'm not letting you out of my sight tonight. Your car will be safe here. Iris is going to keep it under surveillance."

Now Sierra's eyebrows rose. "Going home with you?"

"Yes."

She visibly swallowed, her expression confused. "Hayden, I appreciate the offer, but I'm fine going home by myself. I have a security system, so don't feel obligated or anything."

"Are you fucking kidding me?" He had to rein his temper in at her words. She'd just had a traumatic experience, but still. *Obligated?* He didn't think he'd done a good job of hiding his anger because she paled, making him feel like utter scum. Hayden scrubbed a hand over his face and took a deep breath. "Shit, Sierra, I'm sorry. I didn't mean to yell. I just...damn it, you were attacked. I need you safe."

To his surprise, she let out a low laugh.

"What?"

"I don't think I've ever seen you like this. Or heard you curse like, well, a sailor. Pun intended." The edginess that had been surrounding her seemed to fade a little. "So you're sure you don't feel obligated? Because I—"

He growled under his breath and palmed his keys. "Come on. We're leaving." Not caring what she thought, he took her hand in his. Those green eyes of hers widened, but she didn't struggle. Just linked fingers with him and silently let him lead her to the elevators. He was parked on another floor and couldn't get out of here soon enough. Part of him wanted to take over and lead the internal investigation, but being with Sierra right now was more important than anything.

It was beyond time he told her how he felt about her. If he lost her as a friend...no, he couldn't even go there. He wouldn't. He'd seen flashes of lust in her eyes before but the woman was so damn innocent. He was pretty sure she was a virgin even though she'd never come out and said it. He knew he wasn't remotely good enough for her, especially not if she was actually that innocent, but he wasn't waiting any longer. If she rejected him, he'd deal. If not...he was going to give her the most intense pleasure of her life. And make sure she enjoyed it so much she never wanted to walk away from him.

CHAPTER FOUR

Hayden tensed as he heard Sierra's light footsteps on the stairs. After stopping by her place and letting her grab enough clothes for a few days, they'd come back to his home. He lived in a two-story place next door to his brother in a quiet neighborhood on the outskirts of the city. He loved where he worked but he enjoyed being close to the desert at night. Everything out there was quiet, settled...the exact opposite of how he was feeling at the moment.

Sierra had wanted to take a shower so he'd decided to cook for her while she was upstairs. He'd had to grab chicken from his brother's house next door because he'd had nothing thawed out. He didn't remember making the simple rice and chicken mash up, though—because he'd been fantasizing about what she looked like in the shower. Naked, with hot water rushing over her delicious body. A body he'd fantasized about far too often. He imagined her nipples were—

"Hey, you cooked?"

He turned to find her stepping tentatively into his kitchen wearing green and blue striped pajama pants and a fitted green tank top. Unable to stop himself, his gaze zeroed in on her breasts. She definitely wasn't wearing a bra and he was at the end of his rope pretending he didn't feel anything for her. He simply couldn't do it anymore.

"Uh, Hayden?" Sierra's nervous voice drew his gaze up to meet hers.

She'd asked a question… "Yeah, I thought you'd be hungry." He turned back around and tried to will his body under control. Too bad it wasn't working. His cock was insistently pushing against the zipper of his pants, and he just prayed Sierra hadn't noticed.

"Thanks. Whatever it is smells amazing." She leaned against the counter next to him looking a lot better than a couple hours ago. Except that fucking bruise on her temple that made him want to hunt down her attacker and inflict serious damage. At least her ivory cheeks had color in them again and she didn't have that terrified look. She'd left her jet black hair down so that it fell in damp waves over her left shoulder, covering one breast. God, what he wouldn't give to taste her nipples. To suck on them until they were tight little buds, shiny from his kisses and—

Sierra laid a reassuring hand on his forearm and he realized he'd just been staring. "I'm okay. I hate that worried look on your face."

Hayden cleared his throat and turned off the stove, glad she'd mistaken his expression for worry. Ignoring her statement, he said, "I've got beer and water in the fridge—but you probably shouldn't have anything alcoholic tonight. It doesn't seem like you have a concussion but it would make me feel better. If I'd known you were coming I'd have picked something up. Luckily Jay had a few things at his place." His girlfriend Ellie's influence no doubt.

Sierra just smiled and pushed away from the counter. "I don't think I have a concussion either, but water is totally fine."

As Hayden pulled out plates he looked over his shoulder to find her bent over slightly as she peered into his refrigerator, that pert ass sticking up. The sight evoked way too many hot fantasies and he tore his gaze away with difficulty.

"Oh my god, pretty much *all* you have is beer and water. This is horrible, Hayden." Her sweet voice was chastising. "I would go crazy with a fridge like this. No wonder you're always eating at Cloud 9."

Grinning, he started to set the table. "They've got the best chef in town."

A beer and water bottle in her hands, she nudged the door shut with her hip. "Whatever. You can't live on just dinners of veal *forestiere* or roasted rack of lamb all the time."

"Yes I can. I already do."

She shook her head, but her lips curved up into a soft smile. "That's just sad. You need to take better care of yourself with meals like breakfast and lunch."

"How about I just take care of you tonight?" he murmured, watching her carefully.

Her cheeks flushed a delicious shade of pink as she sat at the table. "Thanks, I appreciate it."

He grunted, not wanting her appreciation.

"So have you heard anything from Jay or Iris? I know it hasn't been that long, but I thought they might have found something." She shivered lightly and Hayden resisted the urge to drag her into his arms and comfort her. He needed to show restraint when she was so vulnerable.

He shook his head as he set a plate of food in front of her. "Unfortunately, no. But give them time."

Compared to the masterpieces she created, chicken and rice was nothing, but it would fill her up and warm her body. So far she'd been handling everything well, but he was waiting for her adrenaline to crash. Before she fell asleep, he wanted her fed. So when she took a few bites but only pushed her food around with a fork, he frowned.

"Is it that bad or are you not hungry?" he asked before taking a sip of his beer.

"It's great, I'm just...I don't know what I am but I'm not really hungry. It's so sweet that you cooked for me. I'm sorry I screwed up your plans tonight though." She said the last part in a rush and he didn't miss the flash of...hurt in her eyes before she masked it.

But that didn't make sense. "Plans?" He'd only had plans with her. Like every other Thursday for practically the past year.

"Your date." She set her fork down now, not even pretending to eat.

Hayden blinked at her. What was she talking about? "I didn't have a date—except with you. It's Thursday."

Now she looked confused. “Oh.”

A few things suddenly clicked into place. “You thought I had a date tonight? Is that why you left the security floor upset earlier?” He’d planned to ask her about it, but then the shit had hit the fan and that had been the least of his concerns.

“I wasn’t upset. I was mad you didn’t just tell me. I wouldn’t have wasted a trip up to the fiftieth floor if I’d known you had plans. But…you really didn’t?” she asked, her voice shaking slightly.

The thought that he might have had a date upset her no matter what she said. He could see it written all over her pretty face. Putting his own fork down, he scooted his chair closer and turned her so that she was facing him directly. He was going to set the record straight. “I don’t know who told you I had a date, but they were mistaken.” Casino gossip was notoriously wrong so he wasn’t surprised someone had come up with that bullshit. Practically everything got twisted out of proportion there. Hell, he’d heard that Sierra had hooked up with two of his security guys and he knew for a fact that wasn’t true. “I haven’t been on a date or fucked anyone since the week I met you.”

Her eyes widened, probably because of his crude language, but he could tell the news pleased her. "Really?"

He nodded.

"Oh." She bit her bottom lip nervously.

"Aren't you going to ask me why?" He intentionally dropped his voice, willing her to take the verbal bait.

"Why?" It came out as a whisper.

He leaned closer, placing his hands on the arms of her chair, completely caging her in. That sweet jasmine and vanilla scent of hers wrapped around him. She licked her lips, probably out of nervousness, but it just turned him on even more. "Because I don't want anyone else but you. I'd rather use my own hand and imagine bending you over my desk while I masturbate than actually fuck anyone else."

Her mouth fell open a fraction at his admission so he took advantage. Going at her fast, he crushed his mouth over hers. There was no finesse in his kisses, just a primal need to possess her as his tongue danced with hers.

For a single moment Sierra tensed, but then she was on him. Taking him by surprise, she grabbed onto his shoulders and slid onto his lap, straddling him. As she moved over his erection, he groaned.

She was compact with the right amount of curves and he loved the feel of her on top of him. Her breasts rubbed against his chest and even with the material between them, he could feel her nipples. Hating that clothes separated them from touching skin to skin, he cupped her backside and stood, bringing her with him.

She instantly wrapped her legs around him, but when he started walking out of the kitchen, she pulled back. He didn't pause as he made his way to the stairs.

"Where are we going?" Her voice shook a little, but not from fear. The hunger in her gaze set him on fire. The potency was nothing compared to the brief little flashes of need he'd seen from her before. Flashes he'd wondered if he'd imagined.

What he saw now matched his own desire. But he needed to be sure. "My bed because I need more room." So much more to do what he had planned. "We can take things as slow as you want when we get there," he said as they reached the top of the stairs. But he hoped not too slow. The need to taste all of her was consuming him.

Those expressive eyes widened but she nodded as she leaned into him. He took her mouth again, holding her body against his so fiercely he tried to order himself to loosen his grip. But he couldn't. Not yet. Holding her like this was too damn surreal. For a fucking year he'd made it a point not to touch her.

Because he'd known *this* would happen. One kiss from her and his control was completely shredded. Pushing open his bedroom door with his foot, he headed for the king sized bed he'd never brought another woman to. He hadn't lived here long before getting a job at the Serafina and after meeting Sierra, he'd known he couldn't be with anyone else.

Not when he wanted her so badly. The thought of touching another woman had just felt wrong. He attempted to be gentle as he laid Sierra on the bed, but it was hard when she kept her legs wrapped tightly around his waist and was grinding against him in the most sensuous manner. If their clothes were gone, they'd be fucking. Not sweet, gentle love making like she deserved. Fucking could come later, but he wanted their first time to be slow.

Somehow Hayden tore his head back from Sierra. Her eyes were heavy lidded and her mouth was swollen from their kissing. Her full lips parted as she watched him. "You want to stop?" She sounded nervous.

"Fuck. No." Yeah, real classy. He cringed at himself, but Sierra just let out a laugh, the sound reverberating through to him.

"Then what's wrong?" Her legs loosened around him as she spoke.

Panic set in that she'd changed her mind. "Nothing. I just want to slow down, which means you can't touch me." His words were ragged and uneven. If she was touching him, he'd fuck things up. Of that he had no doubt.

No, right now was all about her pleasure. Before she could ask him why, he reached up and took her hands from his shoulders. Gently, he guided her hands above her head. With a simple platform style bed set he didn't have a railing for her to hold on to or even tie her wrists to...but he would come back to that idea once she was more comfortable with him. Her fingers touched the smooth headboard as he held her wrists in place.

"Why can't I touch you?" she asked.

Opening himself up to anyone other than his brother was foreign, but he'd already opened up to her so much in the last year he decided to be honest. If she ripped his heart out later, he'd fucking deal with it. "Because you make me insane, Sierra. All you have to do is walk into a room and I get rock hard. I want to be free to touch and kiss every inch of you, but if you're touching me, I'm going to be inside you. Balls deep, fucking like I've wanted to do from the moment we met." He rolled his hips, pushing his cock against the juncture of her thighs with insistency. Man, he wished there wasn't any clothing between them.

She shuddered, her eyes growing even more heavy-lidded with lust. "From the moment..." She trailed off when he possessively cupped her breast. Even though she had a petite frame, her breasts were a little larger than a handful. He gently massaged it, lightly rubbing his thumb over her nipple.

"The *moment.* You're so damn sweet I knew I was no good for you." She started to protest but he placed a finger over her lips. "The only thing I want to hear out of your mouth is 'faster', 'slower' or 'fuck me harder, Hayden'." He'd never been a talker in the bedroom so he wasn't sure what had come over him. Okay, that wasn't true. The most primal part of him understood that Sierra would need this. At least at first. She needed reassuring words and he'd give them to her.

Then he would sink inside her and not stop until one of them passed out from pleasure. "Can you follow orders?"

"Maybe."

"That's not what I want to hear," he murmured.

"Too bad." Her lips quirked up as she slightly wiggled her hips against him and he realized she was teasing.

He pushed out a slow breath. Yeah, he definitely needed to relax. Right now he was wound too tight.

He didn't bother fighting his smile. "No touching," he growled softly before nipping her bottom lip and tugging it between his teeth.

In response, Sierra moaned and arched her back. She moved her hands but instead of trying to touch him, she laid them against the sheets and dug her fingernails into the bedding. She wanted to touch him so bad she ached for it, but damn his bossiness. She would follow his orders. This once.

Okay, the truth was, she'd probably follow any orders he gave her in the bedroom if it paid off enough. The ache between her legs bordered on painful. For reasons she didn't even want to think about, she was still a freaking virgin at twenty-two. That was all about to change tonight. And something told her that Hayden would make this a night to remember. She should probably tell Hayden she'd never done this before, but she didn't want him to stop.

She still couldn't believe how open and almost dirty he was being with her. Sierra loved this side of him. Even though he was one of her best friends, he'd always been respectful of the fact that she was a woman and watched his language. Now he wasn't holding *anything* back. And it was hot.

Hayden's big hands skimmed down to the hem of her tank-top. For a moment he teased the bottom of it before slowly pushing it up. She swallowed hard when reality set in that he'd be seeing her naked soon. Unlike her gorgeous sister and mother, she hadn't gotten any height or their amazing genes. And she definitely wasn't like the tall, lithe women she'd seen hanging onto Hayden at the casino.

"Hey, where'd you just go?" Hayden asked.

Blinking, Sierra realized Hayden was staring up at her. One of his hands was lightly gripping her hip and the other had pushed her top up, baring her belly. "Nowhere."

His eyes narrowed. "Don't lie. Not now."

Showing insecurity was so not sexy but he was right. Sierra didn't want to lie. "I'm just worried you won't like what you see." Even admitting it out loud made her feel stupid, but luckily he didn't.

Sitting up, Hayden wordlessly started unbuttoning his shirt. Sierra held her breath as he began baring so much skin to her. As he slid the shirt off, her gaze tracked over his chest, his rock hard eight-pack of muscles, down to the V... his fingers started working his belt, then the button of his slacks.

She tried to tear her gaze away to see his expression but she couldn't move. It was as if she was frozen, watching him slowly strip for her. Pushing off the end of the bed, he stood at the foot of it. His long, calloused fingers slowly pushed his pants down and she realized she was biting her lower lip in anticipation. He had on black boxer briefs but the visible bulge was huge. It made her suck in a breath. When he finally shoved the briefs down his legs, Sierra's inner walls clenched with unfulfilled need.

He wrapped a hand around his thick cock and stroked once. Her gaze shot to his. His blue eyes seemed almost brighter in the dim room as he watched her. She realized he was baring himself to her so she'd feel comfortable but she didn't want him stroking himself, she wanted to be the one touching him.

Sitting up, she pushed off the bed and came to stand in front of him. She shoved aside her insecurities and slowly lifted her top off. Bare to him from the waist up, she still couldn't shelve the nerves fluttering in her stomach. Until his hungry gaze landed on her breasts.

"Pale pink," he whispered. She didn't understand what he meant until his eyes met hers again. "I've been fantasizing about the color of your nipples for too damn long."

Before she could formulate a response—and she wasn't sure there was one—he dipped his head and sucked her nipple into his mouth. She slid her fingers through his dark brown hair, tightening her grip as he lightly used his teeth.

Too many sensations surged through her. Instinctively she arched into his mouth, wanting more. So much more.

She couldn't believe she was in Hayden's bedroom, doing things she'd fantasized about. And she knew they'd only gotten started.

Grabbing her hips, he moved them backward until she was flat on her back and he was stretched out over her. She didn't have much time to appreciate all that male strength before his head dipped again toward her breast. He let out a strangled groan as he swiped his tongue over one nipple, then moved to the other. Teasing her nipples with his tongue, he licked and laved the hardening buds with erotic little strokes that had her grinding against him.

She might not have much experience but she knew exactly what she wanted. Her panties were damp, her inner walls clenching with a need she knew Hayden would fix.

Groaning, she grabbed his shoulder with one hand and ran her fingers through his dark hair with the other. She didn't care what he said about no touching. That so wasn't happening unless he actually restrained her.

That thought was insanely hot. But only if it was Hayden tying her down. She grew even damper at the thought.

As he continued teasing her, he started blazing a path of hot kisses down her chest, then stomach until he reached the top of her pajama pants. Oh god, he wasn't going to...yeah, he was.

Hooking his fingers on her pants, he snagged her panties too as he tugged them down her legs and tossed them to the floor. Sierra felt a moment of insecurity at being completely naked in front of him, but it vanished when his big body shuddered.

Actually shuddered as he tracked her from her feet up to her face.

"You're beautiful," he murmured before pressing his hands on the inside of her knees, urging her to spread her thighs wider.

Part of her wanted to cover herself, but with Hayden kneeling in between her legs looking hungry for her, she savored being on display for him.

She knew what he was going to do, could see the determined look in his eyes, but nothing prepared her for when he buried his face between her thighs. Her hips vaulted off the bed as he sucked on her clit. The action was sharp and unexpected and sent a punch of pleasure to all her nerve endings. She'd touched herself before but nothing compared to having Hayden's mouth on her most intimate area.

Groaning against her, he pressed on her inner thigh when she tried to close her legs. As he gently teased and licked her clit, he drew one finger down the length of her wet slit. She was so wet she was a little embarrassed. But when he'd told her that he'd wanted her from the moment they'd met, it had turned her on like nothing else could.

When he pushed a finger inside her, her inner walls clenched convulsively around him.

"Fuck," he muttered against her.

She tightened around him, loving the feel of him inside her. Slowly, he pulled out, then pushed back in, over and over, the action rhythmic and wonderful. The way he played her body was perfect and a little maddening. She knew she was close to orgasm but she needed more stimulation. It wouldn't take much to push her over. Her body was primed with the need to come.

"Touch your breasts," Hayden ordered, barely stopping to talk between his strokes.

Cupping herself, she was nervous to touch herself in front of him, but she didn't even think to deny his demand. With her thumbs she began lightly rubbing her already aroused nipples. As he increased the pressure on her clit, her toes curled against the sheets.

"I'm going to come." She wasn't sure why she was announcing it. Lord, her entire body was going into sensory overload.

He made an incomprehensible growling sound that was almost triumphant. When he added another finger to her pussy, her hips bucked against his face as a sharp climax surged through her. Piercing all her nerve endings, the orgasm was way more intense than when she stroked herself.

Her stomach muscles tensed as she rode through wave after wave of pleasure. Grabbing the sheets beneath her, she moaned as he continued his delicious assault until finally it was too much.

She had to push his head away. The stimulation against her clit was becoming almost painful. She was worried he'd be offended, but he chuckled as he pulled back and sat up on his knees.

"That was amazing," she whispered, glad she could actually find her voice. She felt so relaxed she was surprised she'd managed that.

He crawled up her body and brushed a light, almost chaste kiss on her lips. "We're just getting started." That knowledge made her nipples tingle in anticipation. But to her surprise, he pulled back and slid off the bed. Before she could ask what he was doing, he gave her one of his half-smiles. "Just need to grab something from the bathroom."

Confusion settled in before she realized he meant condoms. Of course. Thankfully he was thinking straight because she had no intention of thinking for the rest of the night. All she wanted now was to feel and savor every single sensation of Hayden making her his.

CHAPTER FIVE

Hayden pulled out a box of condoms and breathed a sigh of relief when he realized they hadn't expired. His hand actually shook as he took one out. With the sweet taste of Sierra still on his lips, he was barely keeping himself under control.

But after feeling her tight pussy, he knew they needed to talk first. He'd guessed just from knowing her, but he was pretty sure she was still a virgin after feeling how tight she was. Holding onto the packet, he strode back into his bedroom to find Sierra sitting up with the sheet pulled up to her chest, covering her breasts. He didn't like that at all. But he did like the sight of her in the middle of his bed with rumpled hair and a clearly satisfied expression on her face.

Right where she belonged.

Her gaze tracked to his hard cock, then went to the condom in his hand. When she licked her lips in that adorably nervous way he was used to, he tossed the condom onto his nightstand and sat on the edge of the bed. It was a serious effort in control not to just jump her. He drew the sheet away from her because he wanted to see all of her. Even if the sight of her breasts was a huge distraction.

"I need to ask you something, honey," he said quietly.

"I think I know what and yes, I'm a freaking virgin." Sighing, she fell back against the pillow. Her breasts bounced softly with the movement, making his cock ache even more. Sierra covered her face with one arm and groaned. "Does that mean you want to back out of this?"

"Hell no." Never. He stretched out next to her and propped his head up on one hand while laying his other over her flat stomach.

She dropped her arm to look at him and he saw relief in her eyes.

"How is that possible?" he asked, still astounded. She was a decade younger than him, but twenty-two was still old enough to have had a few lovers. The thought of anyone else touching her made a raw possessiveness rear up inside him but he shoved it down. Now wasn't about that.

Shrugging, she placed her hand over his. He could see the pain in her eyes, but she held his gaze. "It wasn't one thing. During high school the few times I thought a guy was interested in me it turned out they wanted to date my sister."

Hayden's lips pulled into a thin line at the mention of her sister, Shae. He'd met her once and that was enough. She was the polar opposite of sweet Sierra. "I bet she ate it up," he muttered.

Sierra blinked, but didn't respond. She just cleared her throat and averted her gaze for a moment. "I didn't really care that much about the opposite sex in high school anyway. I was so focused on graduating and getting into the Culinary Institute of America and boys weren't important. Then in culinary school I was on the fast track program. The little downtime I had, I wanted to spend with my friends. Living in New York was amazing and there was always so much to do. I guess I'm just not a one-night stand kind of girl. There was never an opportunity." When he frowned she rolled her eyes. "Okay, there were opportunities, I just never took them. I wanted my first time to mean something… Gah, you've totally changed your mind about tonight haven't you?" She started nibbling on her lower lip again.

Hayden's eyebrows rose. "*No.* Why would you ask that?"

She shrugged jerkily. "I don't know. Maybe because I have really limited experience and I know you have...a lot more."

He wouldn't deny that. When he'd been in the Teams getting laid had been easy when he'd been stateside. All he'd had to do was head down to a local bar filled with SEAL groupies and have his pick. Sex had always been about release though. A way to chase away the demons. Until he'd met Sierra. It was like he could divide his life into halves now. Before Sierra and after. "I don't care about that and neither should you. There's no one in my life except you. This thing between us—it's not casual for me." Those were words he'd never said to a woman. Never thought he'd want to say. Until Sierra.

She'd called him on his shit literally the first time they'd met. And the feisty woman had just looked so damn sweet when she'd done it, there'd been no way he could be rude to a woman like her. She was always going out of her way to be kind to people at work whether they deserved it or not. For some reason she liked to see the best in people. She'd definitely seen it in him.

She smiled softly. "Me neither." The exact words he wanted to hear. He pushed out a breath he hadn't realized he'd been holding.

There was such a raw vulnerability in her eyes that it was like a punch to his senses. Sierra was so funny, smart and incredibly talented that her being nervous now surprised him. But after meeting her sister a few months ago, maybe he should have realized. The woman was gorgeous to be sure, but nothing compared to Sierra.

Even though his cock was aching and he had the most beautiful woman naked and willing next to him, for some reason he wanted to talk. *Fucking talk.* He inwardly sighed. Sierra totally owned him even if she didn't realize it yet. Maybe he should shelve the conversation, but he wanted to know everything that made this woman tick. "When I met your sister a few months ago..." Before he'd even finished, she stiffened beneath his hand and went to pull the sheet back up. To cover herself.

Hayden grabbed it and shoved it off her. Now that she'd bared herself to him, there was no way he was losing sight of her sweet body. She made a protesting sound but he rolled over and covered her petite body with his. Her legs automatically wrapped around his hips, pulling him close. He settled against her, savoring the feel of her beneath him, all warm and soft. With his cock so damn close to her pussy it was hard to think straight but he needed to make one thing clear. "A few months ago when your sister blew into town, I saw a side of you that I never want to see again. You were a totally different person when she met up with us. You withdrew into yourself, as if you were afraid to outshine her."

Sierra had been stiff up until that moment, but she snorted. "Outshine?"

Hayden frowned. "Yeah. Anytime I mentioned one of your accomplishments or even talked about *you*, you shut me down. Your sister is pretty, so what? She's also an asshole. You're fucking beautiful inside and out and you're amazing. You're fucking *twenty-two* and head chef at Cloud 9."

Sierra's eyes widened. "I can't believe you just said that."

He rolled his hips, dragging his erection over her belly. He wanted to shift positions and move lower but once his cock touched her pussy, it would be over for him. "You are beautiful."

Now she rolled her eyes, frustration clear on her face. "Not that. I mean about my sister."

He shrugged. "I didn't like the way she treated you. She talked down to you and made you feel like shit. Siblings shouldn't do that. And you put up with it. I…It's why I left early that night. I couldn't stand seeing it and I knew I'd say something I'd regret if I stuck around. Fair warning; if that ever happens again, I won't sit back and watch."

She watched him carefully for a long moment, as if assessing him. It looked as if she might say something, but then she cupped his face with both hands and leaned up to kiss him. Relief slammed into him that she didn't care what he'd said about her sister. If Sierra wouldn't stand up for herself, he damn sure would.

Sierra didn't know when it had happened, but she'd completely fallen for this man. When he'd said this wasn't casual for him, she was relieved but she hoped that meant the same thing for him that it did for her.

But she wasn't going to worry about that. At least not at the moment. No, she was going to take exactly what she wanted. Hayden was right about her letting her family treat her wrong. Growing up with such a gorgeous sister and a mother who placed a priority on looks had taken a toll on her self-esteem. Moving away for school and developing her own circle of friends had made a huge difference in the way she looked at herself. Intellectually, she understood all that but when her sister had stopped in town for a few days, Sierra had felt like that chubby fifteen year old again. It hadn't helped that Shae had flirted mercilessly with Hayden.

He'd barely tolerated Shae. Something that hadn't gone unnoticed. She'd been secretly pleased, and had fallen for him a little more that night. Sierra just hadn't been sure why he'd acted the way he had.

Until now.

As she held his face in her palms, Hayden's hands started roaming her body in a way she'd only fantasized about. After the orgasm she'd just had, she wasn't sure if she could have another but she didn't even care.

She wanted to feel him inside her, to be completely possessed by this man. When one of his hands cupped her breast and began rubbing her already sensitized nipple, she arched her back, pushing into his grasp.

As his other hand cupped her mound and slid two fingers into her slick opening, she felt as if she could combust on the spot. Feeling that thickness inside her made her entire body tingle because she knew soon it wouldn't be just his fingers.

He pulled his mouth back from hers and she started to protest, but his lips trailed down her jaw to her neck and he lightly tugged her earlobe between his teeth all while continuing the soft thrusting of his fingers. When he added another, she instinctively arched her back again, enjoying the fullness of him stretching her body.

Reaching between them, she wrapped her hand around his cock, amazed by the thickness and heat. She wanted to touch all of him, to stroke him the way he was her. Even more, she wanted to pleasure him, to learn his body and what he liked.

He groaned against her ear, the sound almost guttural as his entire body shuddered under her hold. "No touching," he growled.

"I never agreed to that." She barely rasped the words out as she continued stroking him. Just the feel of him in her hand made her feel powerful and sexy.

The hand that had been cupping her breast suddenly moved and encircled her wrist. He sat back so he could look down at her, hunger on his face as he moved her hand away from his hard length.

"This might hurt the first time." He looked so stricken she couldn't fight a smile.

"I know." She didn't care because she knew it wouldn't last. So many times in school she'd worried that she was an idiot for waiting but now she was glad she had. No one could ever compare to Hayden. It just wasn't possible.

His expression softened before he leaned over and snagged the condom. After sheathing himself, he covered her mouth with his. As his tongue danced against hers, he settled between her thighs, his cock nudging her opening. She clutched onto his shoulders in an attempt to ground herself. He slowly pushed into her a fraction, then stopped, letting her body adjust to him.

With his size, she'd worried it would hurt but she was so slick, so turned on, her inner walls were tightening, just waiting to be filled by him.

Rolling her hips, she tried to force him to move deeper but he just laughed lightly against her mouth. His lips trailed lower once again, nipping and teasing until he found her aching breast.

Sierra slid her fingers into his dark hair, clasping his head as he flicked his tongue across her nipple. Almost simultaneously, he began rubbing her clit again in a slow motion designed to torture her, she was sure. His thumb and forefinger increased in pressure when his tongue did.

She shuddered and increased her grip on his head as more pleasure spiraled through her. Tightening her legs around him, she dug her heels into his ass. "I need more, Hayden."

The second she said his name, it was like something in him snapped free. She could still feel him keeping a tight rein on his control, but he finally pushed deeper, giving her what she needed.

Both his tongue and expert fingers kept up their teasing as he pressed into her, then pulled out. He pushed in deeper the next time. In and out, not deep enough to give her exactly what her body craved, but enough to push her right to the edge.

She hadn't thought it possible, but she was close to coming again. "I'm close," she whispered, unable to get out more than that.

Her inner walls clenched tighter and tighter, trying to draw him into her as he tweaked her clit. When he lightly pressed his teeth down on her hard nipple, the sensuous action set off her release.

As her climax slammed through her, Hayden thrust fully inside her. All the breath whooshed from her lungs as he buried himself deep. The pain was fleeting, mixed with the surging orgasm punching to all her nerve endings.

"Sierra," he groaned. Hayden buried his face against her neck, letting out a strangled moan as his thrusts grew harder and more unsteady.

Rubbing her breasts against his chest, she savored all the sensations overwhelming her as she tightened her grip on his head. She felt as if she was holding onto him for dear life as he continued pumping into her.

She felt his heat, his stomach muscles clenching and when he let out a strangled moan against her ear, a raw type of power filled her as he climaxed long and hard. Eventually his thrusting slowed, though his breathing was erratic as he pulled his head back to look down at her.

Staring into those blue eyes, she thought she could drown in them and not care. Before he could ask her if she was okay, she smiled, unable to stop herself. "That was amazing." He was still half hard inside her so she tightened around him, dragging a shudder from his big body.

"Yes it was," he murmured before kissing her lips. Even though the caress was light, it still felt as if he was claiming her in some way and she was more than happy to let him.

She just hoped that wasn't wishful thinking on her part because she had completely fallen for Hayden.

CHAPTER SIX

Hayden traced his finger down Sierra's bare stomach and grinned against the top of her head when she covered his hand with hers to stop him.

"That tickles," she murmured, still half asleep.

She was tucked up against him, her compact body snug and exactly where it should be. The feel of her ass right over his cock was driving him crazy, but it was worth it to have her in his arms. Now that he had her in his bed, he wasn't letting go.

In response he nipped her shoulder with his teeth then followed up with a swipe of his tongue.

"Oh my god, are you a morning person?" she groaned and wiggled against his erection. "Let me sleep, you maniac."

He chuckled, despite the ache between his legs. "It's almost noon."

She stiffened then turned in his arms. Her green eyes were bright with surprise. "Are you serious?"

"Yep." Hayden tightened his arm around her, pulling her close.

Her breasts rubbed against his chest as she wrapped her arms around him, making him shudder. He'd never get tired of the feel of her in his arms like this. It wouldn't take much to slide right into her, but he worried she'd be sore after last night. After their first time together he'd assumed she'd be too sore to do anything else but they'd made love again in the shower a few hours later. Thankfully he'd lasted a hell of a lot longer then. Getting inside her that first time had been electric. He'd felt like a fucking teenager barely able to control himself.

"I can't believe I slept so long," she murmured against his chest as she snuggled closer.

"A lot happened yesterday and we were up *very* late. You needed it." He slowly rubbed his hand up and down the length of her spine, enjoying the way she felt against him.

When he went to cup her ass, she laughed and pushed at his chest. "No. I need to brush my teeth and I'm starving." Almost on cue, her stomach rumbled, which made her cheeks flush that shade of pink that drove him crazy.

He could eat too, though he'd rather eat her. But after the day she'd had yesterday, he was taking care of her right now. The most primal part of him wouldn't allow any less. "Jay dropped off some groceries a few hours ago so come downstairs when you're ready." He threw off the covers and slid out of bed because good intentions or not, if he stayed there, he knew what would happen between them.

A soft smile played across her lips as her gaze tracked his movements. It roved over his entire body in a way that made his cock even harder. Something he hadn't thought possible.

"Keep looking at me like that and you're not leaving that bed."

Her eyes met his and he could tell she was contemplating just that. But…she needed sustenance. Groaning, he dragged on a pair of boxers and hurried from the room. The sight of her naked and willing in his bed was too much for his restraint.

Downstairs he started making turkey sandwiches. He was so thankful Jay had brought food over even if he was a little embarrassed by how bare his fridge had been. If he'd thought Sierra would be coming over he'd have made sure he was better prepared. At least his place was clean.

A few minutes later Sierra came downstairs looking refreshed and wearing one of his T-shirts. And nothing else. She was so petite it fell almost to her knees, covering more than some dresses he'd seen her wearing. Still, it would be so easy to push his shirt up and—

"No way." Sierra stepped into the room with a half smile. Before he could ask what she meant she continued. "After last night I recognize that look very well and I'm hungry and...a little sore."

Guilt instantly flooded him but she crossed the short distance to where he stood at the counter. She went to wrap her arms around his middle and he tugged her close, embracing her tightly. "Sorry, I wasn't even thinking."

"I didn't even realize it until I got out of bed. I think I just need a few hours and I was thinking..."

"What?"

"I called my doctor and she can fit me in today. Since I have the next few days off I'd like to get a prescription for the Pill as soon as possible." She looked almost nervous as she said it. He couldn't understand why.

The thought of getting to be inside her with no condom made him shudder. "I'll take you."

"Really?" She seemed surprised.

"I'm not letting you out of my sight."

Worry slid into her eyes as she looked up at him and he knew she was thinking of the attack. "Have you heard anything from the casino?"

Hayden shook his head as he cupped her cheek and gently turned her face. Anger surged through him at the sight of her bruise. It was a little darker today, a faint purple staining her temple. "They're ripping apart the video feeds, trying to see if they can get another shot of the guy running away and Iris has brought in all new tech guys to comb over the system for glitches or signs of outside hacking."

"It seems like a lifetime ago," she murmured, laying her head against his chest.

"I hate that it happened to you." He slid his fingers through her hair, cupping the back of her head and holding her close.

"I do too, but I'm not sorry about what happened between us."

"Me neither." He hated that it had taken her being attacked to wake him up, but now that he had, he wasn't letting her go.

* * * * *

Sierra tossed a new toothbrush and tube of toothpaste into her hand-held basket. After going to her doctor, she'd dropped off her prescription for birth control at the pharmacist and had decided to wait the hour it would take for them to fill it instead of coming back. Hayden didn't want to wait, but he was just being difficult and it was silly to go all the way back to his house, then come back here. Yes, someone had attacked her at work, but unless he was keeping something from her, she doubted someone was stalking her and she refused to stop living her life.

It was a little odd to have Hayden with her though. She was so used to doing things on her own. "You don't have to hover," she murmured, unable to ignore his giant presence behind her as she tried to decide which shampoo she wanted.

She lightly nudged him with her elbow only to come in contact with pure muscle. He let out a pained sound. Immediately she turned and looked up to find him grinning at her.

Then his expression turned serious. "I just don't like having you out in public."

"It's not like there's an assassin hiding in the candy aisle." She nudged him again when his gaze immediately went in that direction.

He looked back and started to respond when his phone buzzed. "It's Iris," he murmured. "I need to take this."

As he slid his phone out, she mouthed the word 'restroom' and handed him her basket. He started to follow her, but she glared at him. She certainly did not need any help in there.

He held up a hand in a defensive gesture as he answered, but stayed put. Probably because he could see the entrance to the short hallway where the restrooms were.

Sierra hurried, not wanting to take the chance he might actually follow her in. The sexy man had been her shadow all day—which she appreciated. But there were some things she didn't need him for.

As she stepped inside the florally scented room with small square green tiles reminiscent of the seventies, she let out a sigh of relief. Being with Hayden all morning was wreaking havoc on her senses. The man was walking talking sex appeal and he was hers. At least for the moment. She was trying to wrap her head around her new relationship along with the craziness of yesterday. Before she'd taken another step, the closest bathroom door opened and her friend Marty stepped out. He worked in hotel security analyzing videos.

And he was pointing a gun right at her.

It was as if all the air in the small room was sucked out. For a moment all she could do was stare at the weapon and him. "Wh..." She cleared her throat, trying to find her voice. "What are you doing?"

His dark eyes narrowed, his face twisted into an expression of rage she'd never seen on anyone. "You're coming with me, slut."

That word was like a slap to her senses. "What?"

"You heard me," he growled, though he hadn't made a move closer yet. And his gun hand never wavered. Which told her he was pretty damn comfortable holding the thing.

Her insides quaked as she watched him, but she forced herself to remain outwardly calm. After working at one of the most stressful, busiest restaurants in the city, she was used to working under pressure. Of course her only pressure there was the fear of getting fired. Not losing her life. "Why are you pointing that at me? I thought we were friends. And how did you know I'd be here?" She remembered that he was the one who'd told her Hayden had a date.

He rolled his eyes and took a step closer. "I tracked you using your phone. Had to duck in here so your giant shadow wouldn't see me. Didn't know you'd come in here," he muttered. Before she could respond, he covered the few feet between them and grabbed her arm in a vise like grip as he shoved the gun into her side. She let out a tiny yelp of pain as his fingers dug into her skin.

An icy chill snaked through her veins, her entire body growing clammy. Even with the material of her summer dress as a barrier, the feel of the gun against her was surreal.

"You're coming with me." He pressed the gun deeper into her ribs, but she bit back a cry, not wanting him to accidentally shoot her. He pulled open the door and peered into the quiet hallway.

She couldn't see anything because of the angle he was holding her at, but the hall must have been clear because he let out a sigh of relief.

Sierra found her voice. "I'm not going anywhere with you." She was glad her voice didn't shake. She sounded a lot braver than she actually felt. Marty was clearly unstable, but if he'd been smart and determined enough to track her, he wasn't going to just shoot her in a public place. And there was no way in hell she was leaving this building with him.

He turned to look at her then, that look of rage so crystal clear it made her shiver. This was a man very capable of violence. It stunned her. How had she never noticed it before? "Unless you want me to fill you with bullets, you'll do exactly what I say."

CHAPTER SEVEN

Hayden stood at the end of the aisle of feminine products as he waited for Sierra, his phone against his ear. There was a security mirror angled on the far wall so he had a perfect view of the hallway without letting her or anyone else see him. He didn't want her to feel smothered by his presence but he still wasn't letting her out of his sight.

He understood that she wanted to get back to normal and that was why he'd been okay with bringing her to the doctor and now to the pharmacy. Maybe 'okay' was a bit of a stretch, but she couldn't stop living because of one lone maniac.

Or at least that's what he'd thought until what Iris had just said to him over the phone. "Both you and the police are sure Marty is behind this?" he asked. The thought of someone Hayden had actually worked with being involved made him see red.

"Unfortunately yes. He didn't come into work this morning and the outside team I've got combing through his online tracks all point in his direction. Thanks to a weakness in the system he was behind the glitches in the security. Luckily we've been able to create a new patch to prevent this issue from happening again."

That was good, but Hayden was more concerned about what was being done to find this maniac. Slamming Sierra's head into a car could have caused serious damage, potentially even killed her. "What about Vegas PD?"

There was a short silence then Iris cleared her throat. "They've searched his place and...you're not gonna like it, but they found a creepy shrine to Sierra. He's clearly obsessed with her."

Hayden scrubbed a hand over his face. A stalker type. Fucking great. "He wasn't working alone." Marty had been in the security room when the attack had gone down and he'd been the one to cause the glitch. He'd probably expected to be able to cover his tracks immediately. Maybe he and whoever he'd been working with had wanted to abduct Sierra and no one would have been the wiser if not for Jay being there to stop the attack. That seemed more likely if the guy was obsessed.

"Yeah, too bad there's no trace of a partner at his home. The cops are tearing his place apart as we speak, trying to find—"

"Shit," Hayden muttered. All the air rushed from his lungs as he watched Marty step out of the bathroom holding Sierra close. Hayden instinctively stepped back and crouched behind the nearest aisle. He felt as if he'd just been punched in the stomach, but managed to keep his initial spike of fear in check.

"What?" she demanded, her tone sharp.

"Marty just walked out of the bathroom with Sierra. I can't see a weapon but he's got to have one." How the hell had he tracked her without Hayden noticing? Sierra was stiff, her back ramrod straight as Marty dragged her down the hall to where Hayden knew was an exit.

Hayden couldn't see her expression because of the way she was being propelled along, clearly against her will. The man was about five feet ten. With Sierra's petite frame, he towered over her and would easily be able to manhandle her. The guy had to have a weapon. No way would Sierra be walking out with him otherwise.

Hayden was armed and ready. He rarely left home without a gun on his person, but with what had happened with Sierra, he'd made sure he was prepared for anything. "Call the cops. Give them my location." He rattled off the name of the store and major cross-streets before he ended the call and slipped it into his pocket. There wasn't much time to formulate a plan. He had to act now or risk losing the woman he loved.

Marty hurriedly looked over his shoulder, but didn't even glance upward in the direction of the mirror as he headed for the back door. Since he couldn't see anyone he assumed he was safe.

That bastard was about to find out the hard way he was far from it. And if he hurt Sierra, he would pay.

Even though everything inside Hayden was urging him to race after them, he knew he had to play it smart and head out the front, then circle back. If Marty had a partner it was possible the guy was waiting outside and armed as well. Hell, probably.

Hayden rushed out of the front door, quickly scanned the parking lot for another threat then immediately headed west to the quietest side of the building. They'd be in the back by now and he had only seconds to get to her. On the east side there was a pet store. Peering around the corner of the building, he could see the back half of a black SUV peeking out. Behind him there were the normal sounds of the street; cars, people walking their dogs and talking on their phones but all of that faded into the background as he zeroed in on his target.

Calling on all his strength, he sprinted down the side of the building, his legs quickly eating up the distance. Weapon drawn from his ankle holster, he paused at the very end of the building.

"You can shoot me because I'm not getting in there!" Sierra's terrified voice rolled over him.

Peering around the corner, he saw Marty trying to drag Sierra to the back passenger door of the idling SUV. The windows were tinted too dark—illegally so—to see if anyone was inside but Hayden didn't doubt he had someone else behind the wheel.

Only ten feet away and hidden, it was still too far for comfort. Hayden's blood rushed in his ears as he mentally prepared himself for what he had to do. The moment Marty took his gun off Sierra, Hayden was making his move.

He'd killed in the line of duty before and right now, he knew nothing was more important than protecting this woman. His woman.

Marty held a gun pressed to Sierra's ribs but she was still struggling. She dug her feet in, trying to pull away from him. When the back door opened, without loosening his grip Marty moved his gun hand to grab for the handle.

Stepping out from around the corner, he raised his SIG. "Drop your weapon!" Hayden shouted.

Marty's gaze snapped to his, the intent clear in his eyes as he started to raise his weapon.

Hayden took the only opening he might have. No way was he letting anyone take Sierra or use her as a hostage. He fired at Marty. His training kicked in as he aimed and shot right at the man's chest. Three shots right in the center.

He was aware of Sierra throwing herself to the ground as Marty dropped like a stone. Unlike bull-shit Hollywood movies, he didn't fly back through the air, just died where he stood. Immediately Hay-den turned his weapon in the direction of the vehi-cle.

A man wearing a black T-shirt and black cargo pants had his hands raised in the air as he fell out of the side door he'd been attempting to open from the inside. He stumbled and landed on his knees. "Don't shoot! I'm unarmed! I'm unarmed!"

He would believe that after he'd checked the guy himself. "Sierra, kick Marty's weapon away." Hay-den was almost positive the man was down, but he wouldn't take any chances.

He couldn't see her expression because his atten-tion was on the second man, but Hayden watched out of the corner of his eye as she picked up the gun.

The back of the building was clear except for a large green Dumpster. "Keep your hands on your head," he ordered the man as he approached, weapon still trained on him. With Sierra safe and unharmed, all his focus was on this remaining threat. The guy was on his knees and trembling as if he might piss himself. In the distance, Hayden heard sirens as he patted down the unknown man.

When he was sure the man had no weapons, Hayden ordered him to lay face down on the concrete and keep his hands stretched out so they were visible. Keeping an eye on the guy, his weapon still trained on him, he stepped sideways in Sierra's direction. He risked a quick glance at Marty's prone body. Chest wasn't moving and blood was pooling all around him.

Out of the corner of his eye Hayden could see Sierra trembling as she stood there, tightly gripping the fallen gun in her hand. Reaching out with his left hand, he took it from her and tucked it in his waistband at his back as he closed the few feet between them. "Sweetheart, how are you? Did he hurt you?" He didn't want to take his eyes off the downed man for a second, not even to fully give her a visual scan.

"He didn't hurt me but he was going to." She wrapped her arms around herself so he threw an arm around her shoulders and dragged her close, still keeping his gaze on the other man. Marty was definitely dead. The cops would verify it when they got there.

"You're safe now," he murmured, wishing there was more he could do other than stand around and wait.

The sirens grew louder and when he was fairly certain they'd pulled into the parking lot, Hayden tucked his gun away. The man on the ground was still shaking in fear, his face turned away from them so he couldn't see what Hayden was doing.

When the cops arrived on the scene, he didn't want to be holding a gun. Even if he'd done nothing wrong, he knew what would happen if his weapon was displayed.

"We're all going to have to go down to the station and you're going to have to answer a lot of questions. Me too. They'll likely separate us to make sure our stories match but video cameras inside back us up and Marty is already a wanted man."

They'd done nothing wrong but it wouldn't hurt to have video evidence on their side.

She started to ask something but he just shook his head when two uniformed police officers rounded the building with weapons at the ready.

Now wasn't the time to tell her about Marty's obsession with her. She'd get her answers soon enough. And he wanted to get her away from the dead body and into the safety of a police station as soon as possible. He wanted answers about who this accomplice was and what their plans for Sierra had been.

A raw type of rage was pumping through him that he'd never experienced before. Holding her close helped soothe it, but he couldn't get the image of her being held at gunpoint out of his head. Didn't know if he'd ever be able to erase that nightmare.

*****

Sierra jumped at the sound of Hayden's doorbell ringing and almost spilled her wine. It was nearing midnight and she was emotionally exhausted. After spending most of the day at the police station answering questions and filling out reports, she and Hayden had finally been let go. She knew she should go to bed, but she'd been enjoying just curling up in his arms and relaxing. After what he'd done for her, she was worried about him too. He seemed totally fine with killing someone to protect her and she wasn't sure how to bring up her concern for him.

She set her glass on his side table and Hayden slid her off his lap onto the couch. "Who is it?" she whispered even though there was no possible way anyone else could have heard her. He'd received a couple texts over the past hour so she was guessing his brother.

"Either Jay or Iris. Stay here," he said in that familiar commanding voice before leaving the room.

Under normal circumstances she might have argued at his bossy tone but after the day she'd had, she didn't care. And she knew he was just looking out for her.

Sierra heard the murmur of multiple voices then a few moments later Iris and...holy crap, Wyatt Christiansen walked into Hayden's living room holding Iris's hand. Sierra was wearing yoga pants and one of Hayden's T-shirts that was a couple sizes too big. He'd insisted she put it on because he liked her in it, but staring at the mega billionaire she felt self-conscious. He was technically her boss, but it wasn't like she ever saw him. Why was he here? Sierra stood and looked from Hayden to Iris with curiosity.

Hayden immediately crossed back to her and wrapped an arm around her shoulders. His presence was more than comforting. She felt like she could take on anything with him by her side. "Is everything okay?" she asked, looking at Iris. Sierra briefly wondered if she was going to get fired or something. She couldn't imagine why but why the heck was Wyatt Christiansen here?

As if he read her mind, the tall man with midnight black hair and piercing blue eyes gave her a half smile. "I was out of town on a trip when you were attacked. Iris has filled me in on the details and I wanted to assure you that this kind of thing won't be tolerated in any of my casinos. We run extensive security checks, but Marty had never been convicted of anything and there were no red flags. Still, I'm sorry about what happened to you and wanted to let you know that you can take off as much time as you need to adjust to everything and we'll be paying for counseling if you decide you'd like it."

Wow. Sierra hadn't thought that far ahead and she doubted she would need any counseling. She was almost embarrassed to admit that she wasn't sorry Marty was dead. He'd been a monster. But the offer was generous.

Before she could respond, Christiansen continued. "There's no time limit on that offer. If you decide a year from now you want counseling, set it up and we'll take care of it."

"Thank you. That's very kind." Sierra tightened her grip around Hayden, feeling near her breaking point. She just wanted to be alone with him and decompress.

Iris motioned to the loveseat. "Mind if we sit?"

Hayden murmured an agreeable sound then they all sat, facing across from each other. There was obviously more to this visit.

Iris leaned slightly forward, sitting on the edge of the seat. Wyatt leaned back against the loveseat, and Sierra imagined the man would be comfortable anywhere. His hand rested casually at the small of Iris's back in a possessive gesture. "I could have called," Iris said. "But I wanted to let you know all this in person. Hayden has been cleared of the shooting, not that there was ever a fear he wouldn't be. Marty's partner got a lawyer and tried to cut a deal but with Marty dead and since Nevada is a three-strike state—Terry Hess will be going to jail for a long time. He confessed to being hired by Marty to attack you at the Serafina, then to helping him attempt to kidnap you today. About a month ago it seems Marty overheard a friend at Cloud 9 joking with you about..."

Iris cleared her throat, clearly uncomfortable, "...you being a virgin. I guess he became obsessed with you and well, wanted you. He paid Terry a lot of money to help him kidnap you. We'll never know what sent him over the edge but I'm guessing your relationship with Hayden played a factor." She pushed out a long sigh. "Personally, I don't give a shit what that lunatic's reasoning was. I'm just glad he's dead."

Sierra wasn't surprised by the other woman's bluntness. But she wished she could feel more relief. She felt some, for Hayden's sake. She was so thankful he was cleared of the shooting. "Will I have to testify?" She'd do it, but the thought of seeing that man again, especially knowing he was the one who attacked her in the parking garage was intimidating.

Iris shook her head. "No, he admitted to most of his crimes in exchange for waiving a jury trial. It shaved a few years off his sentence, but not many. I don't think he wanted to risk going away for longer than twenty-five years."

Now real relief surged through Sierra. That was a long time. "Thanks for letting us know in person."

Iris nodded and stood, her husband following suit. "Take the next week off. I've already got you covered at the restaurant." Sierra started to protest but Iris shook her head. "I'm not asking. You too, Hayden. I don't want to see either of your faces at the casino unless you're there to enjoy yourself."

To Sierra's surprise, Hayden quickly agreed and tightened his grip around her shoulders. After they said their goodbyes and walked the couple out, Sierra once again found herself in Hayden's lap on the couch.

He nuzzled her neck, lightly kissing that sensitive spot behind her ear. "Even though I want to take you right here, I think it's time for bed. You need rest."

She lightly pushed his shoulder, making him look at her. "You need it just as much as me. But first…are you okay with what happened?"

His eyebrows pulled together in confusion. "I hate what happened to you."

"No, I mean, killing Marty." It felt weird to even say the words.

His expression immediately cleared, but he paused and she could see that he was choosing his words carefully. “I’m not sorry he’s dead and I won’t suffer from any guilt over killing him if that’s what you’re worried about. I did what I had to in order to protect you and I’d do it again.”

She was tempted to ask him if he was sure, but she could see the truth in his eyes. They’d talked about his Navy career many times and though he’d never been able to tell her much about his missions, she realized now that he’d killed in the past. She’d figured he had, but now she knew without a doubt. Considering how much he’d given for his country, she was more than okay with that. Seeing death up close and personal had jarred her and it wasn’t something she ever wanted to experience again, but she didn’t want to talk about that right now. If he could deal with it, she could too. “Okay.”

He continued looking at her, an intense expression on his handsome face. “I love you,” he blurted.

She blinked.

Before she could even think of a proper response, he continued. “I know it’s the wrong time and probably too soon for you, but it’s true. I’ve felt this way for a long fucking time. Since about two months after we met.”

Sierra blinked again. “Why didn’t you say anything then?” The words came out louder than she’d intended, but Lord, she’d been harboring a crush on this man since the moment she’d met him. And she felt the same way too. Especially now.

“I…didn’t think I was good enough for you. I knew you were pretty innocent and I was still trying to transition to civilian life. You remember what I was like,” he muttered.

She laughed lightly. “Yeah, you were kind of a bear to be around.”

“And you were the only one to call me on it. At first I was just insanely attracted to you. You wouldn’t believe the fantasies I had about fucking you at Cloud 9 after hours.”

Sierra’s face heated at his words because she’d had more than a fantasy or two about him too. Probably not as dirty as his though. “I love you too, Hayden. I—”

Whatever she’d been about to say was lost as he crushed his mouth over hers. As his tongue danced with hers, she wrapped her arms around his neck. Thoughts of sleep and the insanity of the past couple days faded to nothing when she was with him. After everything that had happened, she was right where she wanted to be. Safe and in Hayden’s arms.

CHAPTER EIGHT

One week later

At the sound of Hayden's front door opening, Sierra slid the covered pan into the pre-heated oven and pressed start on the timer. She'd done all the prep work early so this would be ready to go as soon as he returned. It would give them an hour and a half until dinner was ready. There was plenty she wanted to do in that timeframe.

She was a gourmet chef, but for the last week he'd pretty much refused to let her do *anything*. Well, unless it involved her being naked, and cooking without clothes wasn't something she was brave enough to try yet. The traditional style beef pot roast was incredibly simple but she'd spiced it up just a little. He ate at Cloud 9 all the time so she had no doubt he'd like the meal.

But she hoped he liked her surprise even more.

"Sierra?" Hayden called out in that voice that made her toes curl.

"In the kitchen." She kept her back to the entryway, but looked over her shoulder, wanting to see his expression. Wearing just heels and a dainty little apron—which she'd changed into after prepping the meal—she'd wanted to do something fun for him tonight. It was a small apron, the square front cut barely covering her nipples and it was all lace and ruffles. Totally impractical for actual use, but she hoped Hayden found it sexy.

He'd had to stop by work to go over his schedule and to head up a meeting regarding next week's security plans. It was standard for him, but for the last week they'd been so wrapped up in each other he had a lot of catching up to do. And that was because of her. Not that she felt guilty or anything, but still...

Hayden stepped into the doorway, his tie loosened and his button down shirt undone at the top. With a bouquet of flowers in his hand, he started to smile then froze, his arm falling limply to his side as he took in her outfit. The apron tied in a neat bow at the middle of her back but he could see pretty much all of her backside.

"Holy shit," he growled.

She loved that she got that reaction out of him. Turning to face him, she didn't bother fighting a smile as his gaze skated over her from head to toe. The way the black and white ruffled apron fell, it just barely covered her breasts. Walking toward him, she'd only taken two steps when he covered the distance between them in long, determined strides.

He dropped the flowers on the table before grabbing her hips and hoisting her up. Familiar with what he wanted, she wrapped her legs around his waist, plastering herself to him as he claimed her mouth in a hungry kiss that had her arching into his rock hard chest.

Surprising her, he pulled back after a few intense moments. Dazed, she blinked. "Why are you stopping?" She'd been thinking about this from the moment he'd left.

"I swore I wouldn't jump you the second I got home." His voice was raspy and oh so sexy.

Sierra laughed lightly. "Why not?"

"I feel like all I've done is keep you naked the last week."

"And that's a bad thing?" Starting to feel self-conscious, she loosened her legs but he reached back and gripped her calves to hold her in place.

"No, I just wanted tonight to be special and...move in with me. Please," he added.

Her eyes widened but her grin grew. "Okay."

Now it was his turn to blink. "Okay?"

"You want me to argue?" It would have happened eventually and his place was huge and...she loved him.

"No, but I had a whole list of reasons prepared why you should."

She let out a bark of laughter. "Always ready for everything," she murmured.

Hayden instinctively tightened his grip on her smooth legs, then slid his hands back around until he cupped her ass.

When he'd seen her standing at the stove practically naked and her ass framed by the opening at the back of the apron, that familiar wave of possessiveness and love had welled up in him. He felt it every time he saw her.

It was jarring, foreign and...perfect. She'd filled a hole inside him he hadn't even realized existed. Making the transition to civilian life had been the hardest thing he'd ever done. Somehow she'd made it easier, just by being herself. He couldn't imagine his life without her. Didn't want to.

Now that he'd finally surrendered to his feelings for her and they'd crossed over from friends to lovers he knew there was no going back for him. The fact that she'd agreed to move in so quickly soothed the most primal part of him. Because he wanted a hell of a lot more from her than that.

He wanted forever. It was too soon to ask the big question just yet, but by Christmas of this year, he was going to make sure a diamond ring was on her left hand ring finger. He wanted the whole world to know she belonged with him.

Too soon, he reminded himself as he skimmed his hands over her bare ass. He shuddered at just the feel of her smooth skin and lightly squeezed her. When he did, she moaned into his mouth. The woman was so reactive and he couldn't get enough of her. He pulled back, and she opened her eyes.

"Bend over the island," he barely managed to rasp out.

Her green eyes lit up with desire at his words. She let her legs drop and though he missed the feel of her wrapped tightly around him, he was dying to take her from behind. For the past week he'd tried to be as careful and gentle with her as he could. But her bruising had almost completely faded and he was hiding behind that excuse anyway. She wasn't some breakable, fragile thing.

Sierra was one of the emotionally strongest women he knew. Yeah, she had insecurities like everyone else on the fucking planet, but she kept it together like no civilian he'd ever met. After the shooting he'd expected…something different from her. But she'd been so composed about the whole thing and that by itself, was hot.

"You're trying to kill me," he managed to rasp out as she bent over the marble island and pushed her ass toward him, grinning cheekily over her shoulder at him.

"You love it," she murmured.

He did. The sexy getup she wore stunned him. He'd never expected to come home and find her wearing nothing but an apron and fuck-me heels. It only reaffirmed what he knew about this woman. She was going to keep him on his toes. Keeping his gaze on her, he slowly undressed. First with his shirt and tie, then his shoes and pants. He'd gone commando because he'd known he'd be coming home to her. Her eyes tracked his movements and each article of clothing he lost, the heavier that gaze grew.

"I'll try and be gentle," he said as he gripped one of her hips and slipped a hand between her legs from behind. He dragged a finger down her slit and found her slick with need.

"I don't want that." Turning away, she let her head fall forward, her inky dark hair falling down her back in seductive waves.

"What do you want?" he asked quietly, smoothing his hand down the length of her spine. With her bent forward in such a submissive pose, his cock throbbed almost painfully. He pressed a finger into her, closing his eyes when she tightened around him.

She didn't respond, just pushed back, trying to get him to move. He slipped another finger inside her tight sheath, loving how she molded around him.

Sometimes he liked to tease her; other times he enjoyed getting her off quickly. Tonight he had a feeling it would be the latter. While he wanted to drag out the foreplay, he needed inside her like he needed his next breath.

"Need in you." He couldn't even formulate a complete sentence.

Sierra didn't seem to notice, just rocked against his fingers, her breathing growing erratic the faster he moved. He couldn't believe how primed she was, as if she'd been thinking about this all day. Maybe she had. God knows he had. He'd hated going into work, even for a few hours.

Without warning, he withdrew his fingers.

She let out a yelp of frustration, her fingers clawing at the marble top. "Don't tease." Instead of sounding demanding as he guessed she intended, her words were breathy and needy.

Feeling almost frantic, he retrieved a condom from his discarded pants and quickly sheathed himself. Until her birth control kicked in, he'd be using these but he couldn't wait to feel her pussy tightening around his naked cock. The thought of being inside her without any barriers was almost enough to push him over the edge, so he reined himself back in.

Until he guided his hard length to her wet opening. Feeling her wetness on the head of his cock was too much.

He pushed forward in one hard thrust. She was so wet, but let out a gasp as he buried himself in her tight body. Though he wanted to move, he was so damn primed right now. He wanted to make her come, wanted to feel her climaxing around him.

Staying buried inside her, he slowly pulled the bow from her apron free. He'd noticed that she was sometimes self-conscious about her body, so the fact that she'd been waiting for him, practically naked under the bright lights of the kitchen, told him how much she trusted him. That she was okay being vulnerable in front of him.

Thank God because he would give anything to make her happy. As the apron strings slid away, he reached up and lifted the part that secured around her neck over her head, letting it fall to the ground.

Sierra, bent over and waiting for him to fuck her. Wearing just sexy heels.

He didn't think there had ever been anything sexier. Yeah, his brain was going to short circuit any second now.

Sliding his hands up her hips and over her ribs, he only stopped when he was cupping her breasts. She was practically trembling, her body shaking with a need he understood all too well. Just lightly enough to tease her, he flicked his thumbs over her nipples.

"Faster, harder," she demanded on a breathless moan.

He wasn't sure if she meant his fingers or his cock and he couldn't make his throat work enough to ask. Strumming one of her nipples with more pressure, he let his other hand slide lower as he started thrusting inside her.

His movements grew harder with each drive into her tight body. Her inner walls clenched around him, growing tighter and tighter the harder he slammed into her. She was so close. He could feel it.

So was he, but he was desperate to make her come first. Tweaking her clit between his thumb and forefinger, he increased the stimulation on her sensitive bundle of nerves with just the right amount of pressure to push her over the edge.

"Hayden." The way she said his name was almost like a prayer as her the orgasm surged through her. Her body shook and trembled and she cried out even more loudly as she came.

He wasn't far behind her, his own climax hitting him like lightning, the pleasure pumping to all his nerve endings until finally he was just blindly thrusting his hips against her. Forcing himself to stop, he gently held her hips as he pulled out.

She made a soft protesting sound but barely moved a fraction while he disposed of the condom. When he was done, he turned her around to face him, pleased by the sated expression on her face. "I love you," she whispered, wrapping her arms around his neck and pressing her soft breasts against his chest.

"I love you, too." He'd never get tired of saying it, either. Holding her and being held by her was the best feeling in the world, and he was never letting her go.

Thank you for reading First Surrender. I really hope you enjoyed it and that you'll consider leaving a review at one of your favorite online retailers. It's a great way to help other readers discover new books and I appreciate all reviews. If you'd like to read more of my work, turn the page for a sneak peek.

And if you don't want to miss any future releases, please feel free to join my newsletter. I only send out a newsletter for new releases or sales news. Find the signup link on my website: http://www.katiereus.com

UNDER HIS PROTECTION

Red Stone Security Series

Julieta Mederos looked up from her computer screen as the bell above her shop door jingled. She inwardly cringed. She thought she'd locked the door. It was ten minutes until closing but as the owner of Julieta's Silk and Lace she could make executive decisions. And it was Friday night, she was starving, and the employee she'd had scheduled to close this evening had called in sick. Again.

Since no one else had been able to come in, she'd been stuck covering. *Again.* She hated to let anyone go, but tomorrow morning she was making the call.

Shoving those thoughts away she smiled at the beautiful couple entering. "Hi, please feel free to shop around and let me know if you have any questions about anything."

The woman was tall, slender and wearing a long, bright print Bohemian-style dress with simple gold sandals. She was truly stunning, the kind of woman Julieta wouldn't be surprised to see gracing the cover of a magazine. She smiled back, her expression tentative. "I saw the hours on your door, are you sure you're still open?" When she fingered the strap of her purse, the giant diamond on her left hand, ring finger glinted under the colorful track lighting.

Julieta nodded, already liking the woman from that one thoughtful question. "I'm Julieta so I can stay open as late as you'd like." She flicked a glance to the tall, blond man standing next to her. He looked like a sexy Viking god. Well, a sexy, angry one. He was practically glaring at her. *Okay then.*

Maybe Julieta's discomfort showed on her face because the woman nudged the male in the sharp black suit next to her. "I'm going to shop and my friend here is going to sit right over there." There was an edge to her voice as the woman pointed to a plush couch next to a glass-cased display of discreet sex toys.

Practically growling, the man went to stand next to the couch, turning his body so that he had a view of the front door and the rest of the shop. As Julieta watched him she realized just how huge he was. Most people were taller than her anyway, but with broad shoulders and a muscular body even a suit couldn't hide, a sliver of anxiety threaded through her veins. She'd never been robbed before, but she wasn't stupid enough to think it couldn't happen to her.

Julieta sold high-end lingerie, but she also sold affordable, quality fashion jewelry and sex toys. Some days it amazed her how many toys she sold. Remaining where she was, she placed her hand on the silent alarm button under the display case. "Just let me know if you need help." She made it a point not to crowd her customers unless it was clear they needed assistance and she wanted to keep some distance between herself and the big man in case he tried anything.

"I actually do need help. My friend Elizabeth Porter recommended this place to me," the woman said as she strode farther into the shop, her gold bangles jangling around her wrist noisily.

"Lizzy?"

Smiling widely, the woman nodded. "Yes. We're new friends actually. I just moved to Miami a month ago and my fiancé works for the same company Lizzy and her husband do."

Julieta let her hand drop from hovering over the silent alarm. That explained the man's military-style stance as if he was guarding or casing the place. She tilted her head to the man standing stiffly in the front of her store. "He's with Red Stone too?"

She nodded. "Yes, but he's not my fiancé. That's Ivan Mitchell. He's my personal guard."

Julieta started to raise her eyebrows then caught herself. "Well I'm more than happy to help a friend of Lizzy's. Our mothers go way back and I've known Lizzy since we were kids."

The woman smiled. "That's what she said. She said she's a couple years younger than you and used to follow you around like a puppy dog whenever your parents got together."

At that, Julieta let out a sharp bark of laughter and rounded the counter, all anxiety about the sexy Ivan dissipating. "I don't know about that, but she was quite attentive."

The woman's shoulders relaxed slightly, her sun-kissed arms a nice bronze. "I'm Mina."

"Nice to meet you. You can call me Jules. Why don't you tell me what I can help you with?"

The woman flicked a glance to the front of the store. Julieta followed her line of sight to see the sexy Viking watching them intently again. She squirmed under his glare. It was like he expected her to pull out a weapon at any moment.

Not liking the way he watched her, she turned back to Mina. The tall woman bent slightly, as if wanting to tell her a secret. "I didn't want to bring him but he insisted on coming inside." She let out an annoyed sigh before continuing. "Lizzy said you sold the best lingerie in town and that you sold fun . . . toys," she said in a whisper. Her cheeks tinged crimson and Julieta bit back a smile.

It was always fun to introduce women to their first sex toys. Sadly for her, toys had been her only form of companionship the last three years. Gah, she couldn't even think about that. Nodding, she said, "Are you looking for solo toys or something you can use with your fiancé? Maybe as a surprise for him?" She was just guessing but she'd gotten good at reading her customers the past couple years.

"Definitely with him. And yes, it's a surprise."

"If we can move your scary bodyguard away from the case up front, I think I've got a few things that might interest you. If you decide you like something, I can have it delivered or you can take it with you today—discreetly packaged. And if you don't find anything you like, I have a catalogue you can check out too."

Relief bled into Mina's dark green eyes. "My fiancé, Alex, is coming back tonight from an out of town trip so I'm sure I'll find something."

Julieta nodded and forced herself to ignore the intent stare from the blond-haired, blue-eyed god standing up front as she led Mina to the display case. She'd met enough judgmental men to last a lifetime, thank you very much. Maybe he didn't like the fact that she sold sex toys. Heaven forbid women please themselves on their own. Whatever his problem was, she didn't give a crap. He wasn't her customer and she didn't have time to worry about it.

DANGEROUS SURRENDER

The Serafina: Sin City Series

Taylor Arenas smoothed a hand down her light-gray, pencil skirt as she exited the main elevator onto her boss's floor. Normally she just wore jeans and a casual top to work, but today she'd pulled out all the stops and actually gone for the business-professional look.

She resisted the urge to wipe her damp palm on her skirt as her heels clicked against the tiled entryway on the tenth floor. The ten-story building in Oceanside, California was non-descript on the outside so that most people didn't know what went on here.

Today she wondered if *she* even knew what Powers Group did. Or whether it was all one big lie.

The glass and metal desk the executive assistant sat behind wasn't occupied. No surprise since it was only six in the morning. Taylor was early for a reason. She needed to talk to Hugh Powers and couldn't wait a second longer. Since he was often in by five-thirty, she had no doubt he'd be here.

And with her all-access card to the building she was one of the few people who could get to this floor without bothering with security. Even if she didn't have the access card she could have just hacked her way in. Which was one of the reasons Hugh had hired her five years ago, fresh out of college. There were only three offices on this floor; two for the owners and one belonged to the head of security, Benjamin Escobar.

With her slim briefcase in one hand, she bypassed the first two and went straight to the last one at the end. This morning the glass walls of Hugh's office weren't frosted over and his door was propped open. But she easily saw he wasn't inside before she'd even neared the door.

As she stepped inside, the door to his private bathroom opened. Since it didn't have a regular door, it was as if the wall opened up. When it was closed it was difficult to see the seam.

His dark eyebrows rose as he looked at her attire. In his early fifties, he was a handsome, fit man graying at the temples with a sprinkling just starting to show throughout the rest of his hair. Even when he was dressed in board shorts ready to surf—and that was as often as he could—he had a regal air about him. "Is there a meeting I forgot about?"

She shook her head.

"Good because I don't think those zombie shoes would cut it." His lips twitched at the corners.

Okay, maybe her heeled pumps weren't business-professional, not with the green and pink zombie teeth design covering the front and the skulls dotting the sides. But they made her feel better, more normal. She swallowed hard. "We need to talk." She hated that her voice came out shaky.

His dark blue eyes filled with concern, which made her angrier. If he was the liar he appeared to be, she didn't want his fake-caring. He pointed at one of the seats in front of his beat up desk. "Sit," he said quietly. The man could afford anything he wanted but he still had the piece of crap desk he'd gotten from a big, box store decades ago before he'd made his millions. She'd always thought that said so much about the type of man he was. He'd never forgotten how far he'd come.

She prayed she wasn't wrong about him. If he was ripping off his own company . . . it would break her heart.

Swallowing hard, she didn't bother taking off her coat as she sat ramrod straight and met his gaze. "For the last week I've been working on investigating those six companies you wanted me to." She had a tendency to ramble when she was nervous so she cut right to the point. "Long explanation short, in the process of my investigation I ran across some files regarding Chemagan." She paused, waiting for a reaction, but Hugh just nodded, listening intently as he always did when she outlined something for him. He didn't seem disturbed at all by the mention of the company. "I visited the Chemagan building yesterday." A new company Powers Group had been funneling money into the past six months. A company that didn't actually exist.

He frowned. "You did?" He seemed genuinely confused.

For the first time in a week Taylor allowed a sliver of relief to slide through her veins. He didn't seem defensive or worried. She nodded and set her briefcase on the desk. She'd taken pictures of the decrepit building yesterday with her phone but had them blown up to 8x10s and printed. She pulled out a stack and slid them across the desk to him.

He looked down, scanned them, then looked back at her in confusion. "What is this?"

"Chemagan. A company you've been putting a lot of research and development funds into the past six months." Or someone was. She pulled out two pages of financials, a condensed version of the trail of money she'd discovered.

"What the hell?" he muttered, scanning the readout.

She could have emailed it to him, but she'd wanted to see him in person, to confront him and to see if he was a crook and a liar. Taylor didn't trust many people but Hugh had given her a job when she was twenty-two and in the last five years he'd become the only father figure she'd ever had. This kind of fraud could bring down his company, everything he'd worked for. And in her experience people weren't just a little dirty. That type of dirty business outlook expanded to all aspects of their lives, like a cancer. She just couldn't believe that he'd been hiding what type of man he was, that he'd somehow fooled everyone, including her.

"This is way too much R&D..." Trailing off, he glanced at the pictures again. He picked up one, his jaw clenching tight. "You're sure this is Chemagan?"

"You've never been there?"

He shook his head. "No, this is one of . . . Neal's projects."

Neal Lynch was Hugh's partner and a man Taylor tolerated because she had to. Ten years younger than Hugh, the two had partnered up over a decade ago, before Taylor had even known who Hugh Powers was.

To her surprise Hugh let out a savage curse. "Thank you for bringing this to my attention."

Taylor shifted slightly in her seat. "Everything is in your name, Hugh."

His jaw tightened again, the anger in his blue eyes palpable. "That bastard . . . All that R&D money has to be going somewhere. We need to find out where. It'll prove what he's been up to. Whatever the hell this is," he said, gesturing to the photos and paperwork on his desk.

Hugh seemed angry but not exactly surprised. "Hugh, has he done something like this before?"

Her boss shook his head. "Not that I know of, but lately . . . he's had some money problems the past year. His divorce and other personal stuff."

Personal meaning his gambling problem, something Taylor was aware of, but she didn't comment on directly. "Are you going to involve the authorities?"

He let out a long sigh and glanced back down at the readout. "Maybe. I need to figure out how deep this goes and who else is involved, then we'll have a better game plan. If it'll effect the company . . . honestly, I don't know that I'll prosecute, but if we can get enough leverage to oust him, he'll be done in business. I'll make sure of it."

She nodded, relief slamming through her now that she knew Hugh wasn't involved. Unless he was the best actor in the world, then she believed him. He'd never given her a reason not to and he was so successful that she couldn't imagine why he would start stealing from his own company. Neal, however, did. "I can help with that." Because she had no problem working to bring Neal down. In fact, she relished the idea. The guy was a creep on a personal level, but stealing from his own company and making it look like his partner did it? Super douche. "Do you mind if I use your bathroom?"

He shook his head and pressed a button under his desk. The door on the wall made a soft snicking sound as it opened a couple inches. Standing, she made her way to the plush room and pulled the door shut behind her. Her hands were still damp with sweat so she washed them, then splashed cold water on her cheeks. She'd been so consumed with worry that she hadn't been able to eat much for almost two days. The jittery effect was finally catching up to her.

As she turned from the sink back to the door, she shook her head at the sight of the panel of four video screens. Even in here Hugh had to be in control. She loved her boss but he was a bit of a freak when it came to security like this. He had a shot of his office, outside the main lobby, in the main lobby and a shot of the hallway outside his office.

She started to exit the bathroom when she saw Neal Lynch in the hallway heading for Hugh's office. *Ugh.* He came in early sometimes too and she really didn't want to see him now. She didn't think she'd be able to hide her disgust of him. When he appeared in the doorway to Hugh's office, Hugh started gathering the photographs.

There was no sound unfortunately so all she could see was their interactions and hear a muffled conversation. She hoped Hugh didn't give them away. She didn't want to give Neal time to start covering his tracks. Hugh took one of the photos and shoved it at Neal.

Uh oh.

"You fucking bastard!" Hugh's angry shout carried through the bathroom door.

Well so much for not giving them away. They needed time to gather evidence against Neal, not tip their hands. Too late for that now.

On screen Neal said something then Hugh shoved another photo at him, right into his chest. *Damn it, Hugh, what are you thinking?* Worry spiked inside her.

Neal said something else, still too low for Taylor to hear. He turned away, leaving, and Taylor breathed out a sigh of relief. They might just have to call the cops on him or at least have security escort him from the building. If they revoked all his access to the company system immediately then she'd be able to gather the evidence she needed, she was sure of it.

Suddenly he whirled back and pulled out a gun from the interior of his jacket. He aimed it at Hugh.

Pop, pop, pop.

Her boss stumbled backward, sprawling on the desk as blood bloomed on his chest.

Oh my god, oh my god, oh my god. Taylor slapped her hand over her mouth. She had to get help, to call someone to—oh my god! Neal stiffened as his gaze landed on her briefcase. He knew she was here.

Run.

His gaze swiveled toward the seamless entrance to the bathroom. With smooth movements he strode toward Hugh's desk.

Taylor hurried toward the other door that exited to the foyer for the executive elevator. Her heels clacked on the tile as she yanked it open. Panic slithered through her veins as she spilled out into the open room that led to Hugh's private elevator.

When he'd bought this building he'd made a few modifications, the executive elevator being one of them.

Without glancing behind her she raced across the open space and punched in Hugh's code. Her fingers shook but she got it right the first time. The doors whooshed open and she dove inside, her heart slamming against her ribs double-time.

She hit her finger against the garage button then the button to close the doors. Come on!

The bathroom door opened, ricocheting loudly against the wall as Neal strode out. "You stupid bitch," he growled, raising his gun.

Taylor dove to the side, trying to hide as the doors started to close. The pinging of the bullets against the metal doors was like rain on a tin roof until the door finally whooshed shut in a rush.

Her heart hammered wildly in her chest as the elevator descended. Only as the door opened into the garage did she realize she'd been shot.

*****

Neal cursed as the elevator slid closed behind that bitch Taylor. She was too fucking smart for her own good.

Think, think, think.

He'd only have minutes to act, minutes to get everything in order, to cover his tracks. He whipped out one of his cell phones as he back-tracked to Hugh's private bathroom and through his office. Ignoring his dead partner's body, he dialed 9-1-1 as he hurried down the hallway.

"9-1-1 operator, what is your emergency?" a woman with a crisp, serious voice asked.

"My partner . . . he's dead. She shot him!" He sounded panicked even to himself as he reached his office. Immediately he started tugging his jacket and shirt off. He had to strip, shower in his private bathroom and scrub off all the gunshot residue from his hands and any on his body. He'd be disposing of his clothes and the gun, which wasn't registered to him. And he'd be pinning everything on her. If it was his word against hers he had no doubt the cops would believe him.

"Who's been shot, sir?"

"My partner, Hugh Powers. I came in to work early like I usually do and found Taylor Arenas in his office standing over his dead body with a gun in her hand. I barely managed to escape. She tried to shoot me too but I was able to make it to our executive elevator."

"Sir, I need your physical address."

After he rattled it off, he said, "I just left him lying there. I need to check on him."

"No, sir. If you're in a safe location you need to stay where you are. I've got officers and paramedics en route now."

"He's my partner, my mentor. I . . . I've gotta check on him. He could still be alive."

"Sir—"

He hung up on her. Later when questioned he'd say he lost service in the elevator, which he hadn't been in. But they'd never know that. He was going to turn the story around so that he was the victim and Taylor the aggressor.

Half-stripped, he sat in front of his computer and pulled up the security feeds. As a partner he had access to everything in the building. Not using his code, but Hugh's, he logged in and deleted today's and yesterday's feeds. Taylor had wanted to upgrade their system so that everything transmitted to an external server, but Hugh had shot her down because he wanted to keep his old-school technology. Very anti-Big Brother, he hadn't wanted outsiders to have access to anything to do with his company. Now the old man's stubbornness was going to let

Neal get away with his murder. The irony made him smile.

Next he turned off the security feed completely. Taylor was a genius with computers so it made sense she'd be able to hack in and erase what she'd done. As soon as he was done deleting the files, he tugged off his pants and balled all his clothes together, hurrying back toward his private bathroom.

Shaking, he scrubbed himself raw from head to foot, taking care with his hands and face, the places that had been exposed. He read enough and watched enough television that he knew gunshot residue washed away easily enough. Getting rid of his clothes would be important though. He couldn't do it now, but he would soon enough. Until then he'd have to stash them . . . Where?

There was an empty conference room on the floor below. He could stash it up above one of the ceiling tiles. That would work, especially since the security cameras were off.

What else . . . shit, he had to make sure there wasn't any blood in the elevator she'd escaped in. He didn't think he'd hit her, but if he had, he needed to wipe up the evidence.

Hurrying out of his bathroom, he was relieved to find his office still empty. The head of security wouldn't be in for another hour but he'd need to call him. First, he had another call to make. He grabbed one of his burner cell phones from a hidden compartment in his desk drawer. He glanced at the clock on his wall. He had maybe seven minutes left. At least it would take the police a few minutes to get upstairs once they made it to the building.

His contact picked up on the second ring. "Yeah?"

"Taylor Arenas is on her way to the police station. I need her to disappear quietly. It needs to look like she's gone on the run. Ten thousand in your bank account today if you do it." He was going to make sure that she died one way or another. Even if she went to the police, they'd believe him over her. They'd have to. And he'd make sure she 'killed herself' over her guilt from taking Hugh's life. He just hoped it didn't come to that. It'd be much easier if she simply disappeared.

"I'm on my way. What happens if I can't get to her in time?"

"Make sure that you do." Otherwise he was screwed. "Call me when it's done." He hung up and turned off the phone before tucking it into the bundle of clothes. He wouldn't be using it again and would dispose of it along with his gun and clothes.

Next he hurriedly got dressed in a spare set of clothes he kept at the office before grabbing Lysol wipes from the bathroom. If there was blood in the elevator he'd clean it. After that he'd call his head of security then go back to Hugh's office. He needed to bend down near the body and act as if he'd given Hugh CPR, make sure the evidence proved that he was telling the truth.

Once he checked the elevator and found no blood, the weight on his shoulders lifted. If she hadn't been shot, that made all this easier. It was a classic he-said, she-said situation. He had another throwaway gun he'd planned to leave next to Hugh's body to make it look as if Hugh had shot Taylor if need be. But it didn't look like that would be necessary.

Dragging in a deep breath, he realized he could still get away with this. He just needed to remain focused and make sure Taylor Arenas disappeared for good.

ACKNOWLEDGMENTS

I owe a big thank you to Kari Walker, Cynthia Eden and Carolyn Crane for reading early copies of this story. Thank you all for your insight! I'm so lucky to have you as friends. And as always, I owe thanks to my lovely readers. You all are amazing and I hope you enjoy this new series!

COMPLETE BOOKLIST

Red Stone Security Series

No One to Trust

Danger Next Door

Fatal Deception

Miami, Mistletoe & Murder

His to Protect

Breaking Her Rules

Protecting His Witness

Sinful Seduction

Under His Protection

Deadly Fallout

Sworn to Protect

The Serafina: Sin City Series

First Surrender

Sensual Surrender

Sweetest Surrender

Dangerous Surrender

Deadly Ops Series

Targeted

Bound to Danger

Chasing Danger (novella)

Shattered Duty

Edge of Danger

A Covert Affair

Non-series Romantic Suspense

Running From the Past

Dangerous Secrets

Killer Secrets

Deadly Obsession

Danger in Paradise

His Secret Past

Retribution

Merry Christmas, Baby

Paranormal Romance

Destined Mate

Protector's Mate

A Jaguar's Kiss

Tempting the Jaguar

Enemy Mine

Heart of the Jaguar

Moon Shifter Series

Alpha Instinct

Lover's Instinct (novella)

Primal Possession

Mating Instinct

His Untamed Desire (novella)

Avenger's Heat

Hunter Reborn

Protective Instinct (novella)

Darkness Series

Darkness Awakened

Taste of Darkness

Beyond the Darkness

Hunted by Darkness

Into the Darkness

ABOUT THE AUTHOR

Katie Reus is the *New York Times* and *USA Today* bestselling author of the Red Stone Security series, the Moon Shifter series and the Deadly Ops series. She fell in love with romance at a young age thanks to books she pilfered from her mom's stash. Years later she loves reading romance almost as much as she loves writing it.

However, she didn't always know she wanted to be a writer. After changing majors many times, she finally graduated summa cum laude with a degree in psychology. Not long after that she discovered a new love. Writing. She now spends her days writing dark paranormal romance and sexy romantic suspense. For more information on Katie please visit her website: www.katiereus.com. Also find her on twitter @katiereus or visit her on facebook at: www.facebook.com/katiereusauthor.

15202644R00079

Printed in Great Britain
by Amazon.co.uk, Ltd.,
Marston Gate.